Christmas
at
Holly Berry Cottage

Christmas at Holly Berry Cottage

A SUGARPLUM FALLS ROMANCE

JENNIFER GRIFFITH

Christmas at Holly Berry Cottage

ISBN: 9798561824371

This is a work of fiction. Names, characters, places, and events are creations of the author's imagination or are used fictitiously. Any resemblance to actual persons, living or dead, events, or locations, is purely coincidental.

Cover art by Blue Water Books, 2020.

*For my sisters, Carrie and Adrienne,
and our most fun Christmas singing
trio*

"The earth has grown old with its burden of care, but at Christmas it always is young

The heart of the jewel burns lustrous and fair, and its soul full of music breaks the air

When the song of the angels is sung." –Phillips Brooks

Chapter 1

Chelsea

C helsea Sutherland tidied the Christmas sheet music. She pressed three chords on her piano in succession, and sang the holiday lyrics—alone.

Wyatt was late. Again. After ten years in the trio with him she should have been used to it. If he weren't so charming and easy-going, she probably wouldn't put up with it.

Heath, however, would snarl. In fact, her brother might be snarling at both Chelsea and his lifelong best friend Wyatt right now, two hours away from Sugarplum Falls at his apartment in Caldwell City. He'd texted to say he was waiting for Chelsea to patch him in on a call so they could practice for the umpteen community Christmas events Dad had booked for them to perform.

Sutherlands did love their community events—from the Waterfall Lights, to the Hot Cocoa Festival, to the town Christmas play, to summer nursing home performances, Christmas Tree-O was slated for them all, thanks to Dad's enthusiasm for supporting the community.

She spelled the word *L-A-T-E* on the Scrabble game at the table, then took one of the mugs of hot water with lemon juice and honey from the top of the piano and sipped it. Singer's Tea. It prepped the throat for singing, which she may or may not be doing tonight, if Wyatt didn't show up soon. She had work responsibilities to catch up on, and another family event later. Their practice time window was closing.

"I'm here." The front door of her cottage creaked open, and through it poked Wyatt's head. "You're already at the piano?" The rest of him came in, all six feet of his tall, dark, and handsome relentless charm. Unpunctual

1

relentless charm. "Is Heath steaming as much as that cup of whatever you're holding?"

"Here. I made you one, too."

He strode over and took the cup, his fingers brushing hers before sipping it. "Mmm. You left out the ginger."

"You do hate ginger." Especially in Singer's Tea. "I'll see if I can get Heath patched in." The wireless connection wasn't always the greatest there at her cottage outside of Holly Berry House near the edge of the woods. It'd be so much less of a pain if Heath would just drive over to Sugarplum Falls for at least one practice before they had to run the gauntlet of holiday events they were booked for entertaining at.

Wyatt unbuttoned his jacket and tossed it over the back of a dining room chair, like always. "I brought your mail. I was up at the house, and your mom asked me to drop it off." The envelopes and magazines slapped against the antique wooden tabletop. "It's not all bills. You're lucky."

"Any Christmas cards?" she asked, but a crackly voice interrupted.

"Hey, guys." Heath's face appeared on the computer screen. "You're late, Wyatt."

"Yes, but I brought your sister's mail, so I'm forgiven. She always forgives me when I do a little nicety for her."

"Keep your niceties to a minimum." Heath and his big-brother sternness. "Now, because you're late, I only have seven minutes before I have to leave with Odessa for her Lamaze class, so let's get cranking."

Good. Finally.

Chelsea parked herself at the piano bench and flipped through one of the binders containing their repertoire of bubble-gum Christmas pop.

"Since I'm out of town, let's keep everything as easy as possible this year." Heath took charge, as always. "As usual, I'm on lead. Wyatt and Chelsea, you're on harmonies. Start with 'Holly Jolly Christmas,' and then move through 'Rockin' Around the Christmas Tree,' and 'Santa Claus is Comin' to Town.'" As lead, Heath also made the decisions. It was easier that way, since Chelsea was the younger sister, and Wyatt was too chill to bother challenging Heath's dominance. Sometimes it seemed like Wyatt only sang in

Christmas Tree-O to keep Heath happy.

And probably for all the girls who mobbed him after every performance, batting their eyelashes and asking if he'd autograph something for them.

Minor celebrity status in Sugarplum Falls had its perks, at least for the guys of the group, if not for Chelsea. In fact, Heath had met Odessa after their performance at the Waterfall Lights event two years ago. Now they were married, and any day now Chelsea would become an aunt for the first time at age twenty-six.

"Let's run through 'Holly Jolly' to start." Heath's voice cut out as the image of his face fizzed. "Hav- holl- Chri-" came through in crackling zaps. "Hey, why aren't you guys coming in? Chelsea, you're supposed to harmonize, remember?"

"You're cutting out, man." Wyatt took a gulp from his mug. "You gotta sing louder."

"If I sing any louder, I'll wake the baby inside my wife's abdomen. Now, let's go."

But it wasn't any use, as the connection worsened, no matter what Chelsea did to rejigger it. Her tech skills failed for once, and their practice ended without a single full run-through.

"Bye, guys. I'll"—crack, snap, pop—"Cocoa Festival, if I can." Heath disappeared from the screen.

Wyatt's head snapped and his gaze met Chelsea's. "Did he just say *if I can?* What's that supposed to mean?"

"It means that as long as Odessa doesn't have the baby, he'll trek over to Sugarplum Falls for the Hot Cocoa Festival on Saturday night."

"No whammies." Wyatt set his mug down.

"He'll be there. He's just nervous," she said. "New dad stuff."

Though, Odessa wasn't due until Christmas day. Heath was being flaky.

"Maybe we should run through our parts." She played the full chord, but Wyatt patted her shoulder and went to the table.

"Nah, we know it well enough." He picked up her mail and sank down on her vintage sofa with its nubby red and green plaid fabric. "Junk mail, junk mail, catalog." He tossed the successive pieces into a new pile on her coffee table. "You actually buy anything from this?"

"It's addressed to the cottage resident." She yanked the non-essentials away, creating order from the chaos he was creating in her room. "It probably comes because of Grandma."

"Your grandma died a long time ago." Ten years ago, or more. "And she's still getting catalogs?"

"Catalog databases don't know that." And Wyatt didn't need to know that Chelsea had ordered a pair of cute puppy-face socks from that catalog to keep her feet warm. The Holly Berry Cottage could get drafty. "They're ones and zeros."

"Like the statistics you work with all day?" Wyatt kept snooping through the stack, tossing sweepstakes offers and gardening supply catalogs hither and yon. "You have rescued those big pharma beggars so many times. Are they ever going to promote you?"

"Someday, maybe." She'd only been there about a year and a half. "I don't want a promotion now." Didn't deserve one yet. Nice that he kept track of her life's goings-on, though. Sweet. Better than any other guy she'd ever spent time with. She gathered up another sorted stack and whisked it into the trash can. "I like working remotely where I can control my environment." And help local family members as their *I can't get my document to open* resource.

"And wear pajamas all day." Wyatt smirked at her gray sweatpants.

"These are not pajamas." Even though they did closely resemble her gray pajama pants. Those were fuzzier. "You're just jealous because you're forced to wear a suit and tie to North Star Capital every day, and I get to be comfortable."

Okay, slovenly was probably a better word for it. But she had her reasons for looking this way to solve everyone else's math problems. Good ones.

"Yeah, whatever." Wyatt tugged a cream-colored envelope from what remained of the mail stack and began tearing it open. "Hey, what's this? Somebody is splashing out on very nice envelopes for the Christmas cards this year."

Chelsea reached for it. "You do know that opening other people's mail is a federal offense."

4

"No, stealing other people's mail is." He passed it to her.

She pulled the card and photo out of the linen envelope with a *nyah, nyah* in his general direction.

However, the second she saw the contents, she dropped them like hot coals.

Mr. Sheldon and Mrs. Lisa Lang announce the marriage of their daughter ...

Oh, no. It couldn't be. Not Esther. Not with Fargo. This was too cruel to be real.

"Are you okay?" Wyatt picked up the piece of embossed card stock from atop her puppy-face sock where it was burning her toe. "You look like you've seen a ghost."

More or less. "I wish they'd both expire and *become* ghosts this very moment." Before they could invade Chelsea's world and haunt her entire Christmas season.

"Is that any way to speak about a Sutherland cousin?" Wyatt glanced down at the photo in his hand. "Oh, never mind. It's Esther. I get it."

No, he most certainly did not get it. "Esther is only half the horror."

Wyatt looked closer. "Let's see." He mumbled the details on the invitation under his breath. "Mr. and Mrs. Frye cordially ... the last Saturday before Christmas, nuptials, twenty-two hundred Poinsettia Drive, RSVP ... So?" Wyatt looked at her. But then his arm dropped at his side. "Just a second. This isn't *Fargo* Frye, is it?"

Chelsea nodded.

"Your useless college boyfriend? Heath told me all about him."

Um, not all about him. Nobody but Chelsea knew *all* about Fargo Frye and the decimation he'd inflicted on her life that last semester before Fargo graduated and Chelsea earned her degree in mathematics and statistics. "One and the same."

Wyatt's upper lip curled. "Well, he's getting what's coming to him if he's marrying your cousin Esther."

"That's one way to look at it." But still, it burned like a cinder in her eye. Her horrid ex-boyfriend was marrying into her family, marrying her meanest

5

cousin, even if they had been best friends when they were small, and Chelsea would have no excuse to avoid it.

Esther Lang, hairdresser to the starriest stars in all of Caldwell City. To hear her tell it, she was practically an A-lister herself. "Honestly, Wyatt. I just can't take it."

"Allow me to do the honors, then." He chucked the card in the trash can. "Skip it. Then you don't have to watch the staging scene for the mutually assured destruction live and in person."

"Hey." Chelsea reached into the can and sifted through the Christmas sale coupons and glossy offers for porcelain cat figurines to grab out the invitation.

"Why are you getting that out?" Wyatt went back over to the piano and set his mug on top—not on the coaster. "Forget it."

Forget? As if. As if she'd forgotten about Fargo Frye and what he'd done to her for even one single day since their breakup a year and a half ago. Oh, what a fool she'd been.

Couldn't Chelsea just sink to the bottom of Lake Sugar instead?

"Stop looking for it." Wyatt tugged it away from her again and sent it Frisbee-sailing to the trash can. "You're being a glutton for punishment."

"It's not like I can skip attending it." She plucked it from the trash and set it on the table.

"Of course you can. It's a last-minute holiday wedding, and everyone is really booked up at the holidays. They can't expect you to change plans around them. You're busy. You have a life. Lots of musical commitments to boot. You're not indebted to them, and certainly not to Fargo Frye, of all people."

Yes, she was. Indebted for her complete lack of self-confidence, for her lack of desire to date, for her year of hibernation, thank you very much. "It's a Sutherland wedding. I'm a Sutherland."

Wyatt looked unmoved. "Sutherlands always have plans. You have plans. Just attend whatever plans you already have in place. Give your regrets. Send a chintzy gift. In fact, re-gift something tacky. Or buy them an impersonal gift card in a low dollar amount to a restaurant you know they'd both hate. Just get it over with and then skip the personal appearance. That's what I'd do."

That probably was what Wyatt would do, but with more flair than

Chelsea would be able to muster under the circumstances. "It's at twenty-two hundred Poinsettia Drive. Does that address ring a bell? My parents' house?"

Fifty yards away from where Chelsea lived in the property's original cottage was Holly Berry House, where Chelsea grew up.

"In fact, I'll likely get roped into helping decorate for the thing, as part of Sutherland solidarity. Which is usually a beautiful thing. Just not in this instance."

"Tell me something, then. Why are you just finding out about it?" At this, Wyatt blinked madly. He had thick, dark eyelashes for a guy. So unfair. "Don't you think your mom would give you a heads up if you were expected to be there? Surely they know you're not going to want to subject yourself to it. They only sent you the invitation to be polite."

Good point. He made such a good point. Chelsea pulled out her phone and dialed. "Mom, there's a wedding planned at your house? How long has this been on the books?"

"Esther's scheduled church ended up with bats in the belfry. There was a remediation closure at the last minute, so I volunteered the house, which she said she'd wanted to use for her reception in the first place. Lisa is thrilled."

Of course Mayor Lisa Lang was thrilled. Holly Berry House was the best place on the planet to have a daughter get married, if you were a Sutherland. In fact, Chelsea had always dreamed of her own reception being held there, with the grand staircase bedecked with garland, blazing hearths, steaming hot cocoa scents from the kitchen—and music. Lots of music wafting through the rooms.

"You're volunteering the house for a wedding. Right before Christmas. With zero notice."

"I'd do anything for Aunt Lisa and Uncle Sheldon, they've been so good to us." Mom did love her sister-in-law. So did Chelsea, for that matter. Aunt Lisa was pushy but loving, and one of Chelsea's biggest cheerleaders. *Unlike her sour daughter.* "Uncle Zeke just finished divinity school and will perform the ceremony."

"Zeke, Zeke, the Black Sheep? And he finished divinity school?"

"Finally something complete. We couldn't *not* reward that by including him. In fact, it'll be all in the family, and such a joy to have every single person

7

in Grandma and Grandpa's posterity there. No empty chairs. They'll be smiling down from heaven."

No empty chairs? Not even Chelsea's? That sealed that. She looked up at Wyatt after hanging up.

"I heard." His chin wrinkled in a frown.

Seeing Fargo again, for the first time since he so ruthlessly tore her self-worth apart, and him all starry-eyed over none other than Esther? Chelsea squeezed her eyes shut and pulled her head down, turtle style, into her bulky, misshapen sweater.

What am I going to do?

Chapter 2

Wyatt

Wyatt North sat at his desk and stared out the window at the falling snowflakes coating the sidewalk and shrubbery at North Star Capital—enough that there'd been an avalanche in the canyon between Sugarplum Falls and Darlington, according to the news reports. His pencil eraser tapped incessantly. For whatever reason, he couldn't shake the image of Chelsea freaking out last night.

Chelsea Sutherland did not freak out.

Chelsea Sutherland was the coolest, most logical-minded person in the world. She could calculate risk and assess potential outcomes and see them for what they were. For instance, Chelsea almost never got nervous before Christmas Tree-O performances. *The worst that can happen is they'll boo us off the stage or throw rotten fruit. Meh. Low hazard. I'll risk it.*

Another example. On the morning she was supposed to go take one of those standardized tests to get into college, she'd spent the night before playing video games with him and Heath at their college apartment, and she didn't even bat an eye when they dropped her off without sleep to take the exam.

Which she had aced. Because she knew her stuff. Nothing fazed her.

For that reason, there had to be more to her meltdown over the wedding invitation last night. Sure, Fargo was an ex, and a lame one, but—

"Hello? Wyatt? You in there?" A finger tapped the center of his forehead, and Mack loomed over him, his jowls flapping. "I've been hollering at you for thirty seconds."

Not even. "Hey, my friend. Is the bank on fire? Somebody put too many lights on the Christmas tree?"

"Ha. No, but you'll probably wish." Mack stretched his arms way up, and his shirt came untucked, revealing a good inch and a half of his stout, white belly. "Your parents want to see you in your dad's office."

Very few words in this life could make Wyatt's heart seize. Those were eight of them, however. Mom and Dad were not the most easy-going people to be in a family business with.

"On it." Out the door in a flash, he straightened his tie and lengthened his stride toward the North Star Capital executive suite.

Mack dogged his heels. "What were you daydreaming about back there? Meet another girl at one of your singing gigs? You've got to stop slumming. Your mother isn't going to put up with it for much longer." He laughed his signature *ho-ho-ho* Santa-like laugh.

"Thanks for the tip." His mother's unending disappointment was not the thing Wyatt wanted to think about when he was being summoned to meet Dad. "I'll handle that aspect of my life, thanks." Pretty much anything else, Wyatt would gladly ride out the waves on. Dating, though, he didn't need any commentary from anyone on. Not even Mom.

"You always say that, but she never ceases to make lists that she wants me to float to you."

"Lists."

"Yeah. Lists of gorgeous, available women who have ties to serious wealth."

I know. I know. Mom thought a banking alliance could take North Star Capital to the next level. Dad might think so, too. All of those women, however, had nothing more than dollar signs as the little glint in their eyes.

"Dad." Wyatt slipped into Dad's huge corner office, clicking the door behind him and shutting out Mack's patter. "Mack said you wanted to see me in person."

Dad looked up over the top of his reading glasses, every silver hair in place, as always. "Ah, Wyatt." He set down the file folder he'd been reading. "Sit down."

Wyatt went for the large leather chair directly across from Dad, but Dad indicated the smaller one to the side of the desk, saying. "Your mother will be joining us shortly."

Sans approved-dating list, please.

Wyatt took the lesser chair. "What's up?" He affected a carefree pose, crossing his ankle over his knee. He leaned back, lacing his fingers behind his head. "You looking for a musical group to perform for the staff Christmas party? Because you'd better get your request in soon. Christmas Tree-O's schedule is filling up." Really, he shouldn't purposely bug Dad, but sometimes it broke the ice. "But I can put in a good word. I know a guy."

"Heath Sutherland takes up entirely too much of your time, even now that he's married." Mom stepped into the room with broad strides, settling herself into the queen chair. "I thought it would end when he moved away, or when he married that poor orchard-owner's daughter, but unfortunately we can't seem to rid ourselves of him no matter what."

Poor orchard owner's daughter? Ha. By *poor,* Mom could mean either pathetic or lacking funds. Odessa was neither. Kingston Orchard was one of the biggest employers in all of Sugarplum Falls, and a main engine of the local economy. Mom was just peevish toward anything *Sutherland.* Geez, forgive already.

"That's not why you're here." Dad placed his elbows on the table and steepled his fingers. "It's been a long time coming, but we're ready to give you this opportunity."

Music from that shark movie played in Wyatt's head. "My own investment account." He didn't need any elaborate explanations. This had been promised him since he came on board as a junior executive at North Star Capital five years ago, so he knew the drill. "To use the firm's funds as I see fit, and to test my instincts."

Dad nodded. Mom coughed behind her hand. Wyatt deserved the cough, frankly, at least from what he'd ever let Mom see of his work. If anything really good came of it, he always made it look like Mack or someone else had been the driving force in the deal. It was easier that way than accidentally raising Mom and Dad's expectations of his skill.

Probably not the best way to get ahead in the company, or in Mom's estimation.

But this time it mattered. This time he could see a clear path to the vice presidency of the firm. *Until I'm there, I won't be able to steer the North Star ship back to its original purpose.*

He had to do this right. It was the opportunity he'd been waiting for. *If I can crunch the right numbers.* Instincts? He had those in spades. But math skills, looking at hard data and making informed, wise decisions? Nope. He was still just as bad at math as he'd been when he let down the whole school in the regional Mathletes competition. Mom seriously shouldn't have pushed Principal Sutherland to put Wyatt on that team.

And nothing had improved since.

This challenge, no matter how vital, might be out of his reach.

"You know we're counting on you. We want nothing more than to elevate you to a senior executive level and position you to someday run this firm."

Wyatt wanted it too, if on his own terms. But first there was this massive hurdle to overcome. "I'm on it, Mom and Dad. You can count on me to do what's best for North Star and for Sugarplum Falls."

"North Star comes first, son. Remember that." Mom's glower could melt bricks.

"Good," Dad said, ignoring Mom. "You understand. Now, all that remains is the amount, and it's already in writing and is being couriered to your desk as we speak."

Dad nodded his dismissal, so Wyatt stood to go.

Mom lifted a finger. "Another thing, Wyatt." Her fingernail was a perfect length and painted luxury-goods red. "You're meeting Rowena Gustavson for dinner tomorrow."

"Who is that? An investor?"

"An investor in your future."

Oh, another blind date. "Sorry, Mom. I have plans for tomorrow night."

"They'd better not involve singing in public. If that's the case—"

"See you guys later." He headed out the door and down the hall as if he were going after the Olympic speed-walking gold. Sprinting would have been better. *No Rowena Gustavsons for me.* Or any of the other heiress types Mom continued to dig up for him.

When Wyatt returned, Mack was waiting in Wyatt's office, pacing and humming Christmas music. "You're back. Was that meeting what I think it was?"

A file folder lay open on Wyatt's desk. "You don't need to ask. You already looked."

"Don't blame me. That folder wasn't marked confidential." Mack plopped down in a chair and put his feet up on the broad radiator, nearly knocking over one of the potted poinsettias lining the sill. "Besides, you were going to tell me the second you came in anyway."

True, but not until after Wyatt had looked at the numbers of his parents' focused list of suggested investment opportunities.

Even the thought of having to crunch all those numbers built a snow fort around his will to work. "Tell me something, Mack."

"If your question is whether I think you should invest in Caldwell General Hospital, as it is a listed option in that file there? No. That's a hard no. From what I hear through my second cousin who's in the obstetrics department there, that place is sinking in mismanagement. Cross that possibility off the list, pronto."

Good to know. But that wasn't the topic Wyatt needed insider information on. "You're related to the Sutherlands, Mack. What do you hear about a guy named Fargo Frye?"

"The one marrying Esther Lang?" He shook in the involuntary Esther-was-mentioned shudder. "Besides that he's a glutton for punishment and should get his head examined?"

"Besides that. More specifically, dating history. Did he date, say, any other Sutherland women in the past?" Of course, Wyatt knew the answer was yes, so he might as well state it outright. "I mean Chelsea."

"That's right. Oh, my word. That's the same Fargo Frye."

How many could there be? "Yeah. Same dude. Do you know any of the history?"

"You're the one who should know. You spend more time with her in that singing group than anyone does."

True, which made his not knowing about her situation all the more awkward. "Let's assume I don't have that information."

"Why don't you just ask her yourself? Or ask Heath?"

13

Because they'd hold back, and Wyatt wanted the full scoop. "Your information is more reliable."

Mack puffed up his chest. "That's true. People tell me everything." They shouldn't, since Mack was the incarnation of *loose lips sink ships*. But in this case Wyatt wasn't complaining. "Well, more precisely, they tell my wife everything, and she tells me."

Oh, so that's how it worked. "Anyway, go on. Why did she dump him? Was he cheating on her?" It had to be something like that. The Fargo Frye that Wyatt had met at a bankers conference last summer dripped with infidelity. Okay, that wasn't fair. But the leering eye and the cocky jut of the chin Fargo had given every cocktail waitress at the conference's first-night reception had made Wyatt suspect. "I mean, they weren't married, but two-timing or whatever?"

Slowly Mack shook his head. "I don't think that's how it went down. In fact, I don't have all the details, but I do recall that Chelsea wasn't the dumper."

The other way around? What kind of a medieval dimwit would dump the smartest girl in the college? Or, make that the history of the college? Because that was Chelsea Sutherland. Numbers were her language, and that was only the tip of the iceberg of her genius. "I find that very hard to believe."

"Nevertheless." Mack shrugged. "Why the sudden interest in Chelsea's dating history? Don't tell me you're interested in dating her. Because you and I both know Heath Sutherland would put on his older brother oven mitts and push you into the fiery furnace if you looked wrong at his little sister. And by *looked wrong*, I mean looked at her at all in *that way*."

Oh, Wyatt hadn't looked at Chelsea in *that way* in a lot of years, although there had been a few times back then when he'd been all but puppy-dogging after her when she was around eighteen and he came home from college and sang with her. She'd worn that burgundy-colored dress, and ...

No.

Heath knew Wyatt's dating history. The whole family knew. They knew about Wyatt's stupid every-single-cheerleader thing. Mistakes were made.

One instance they didn't all know but Heath never let Wyatt live down was the time he'd said yes to the nice girl in college for the girls' choice dance and then ditched her for a second girl who asked him.

There were a lot of things Heath didn't know about that situation.

"I'm just concerned about her is all. Chelsea's a friend." Maybe his best friend, now that he thought about it, since Heath had abandoned them for adulthood. "And if her ex-boyfriend is marrying her snobby cousin, I just ..." What? Want to protect her?

Kind of.

Not that being protective or the conquering hero had ever been Wyatt's role in the screenplay of life. Instead, he was typecast as Good-time Charlie. More like the hero's sidekick. The plucky comic relief. The guy who came in and calmed everyone down after a battle, who told the joke to end the scene.

If Esther were to take a true-to-self role for a screenplay, she'd be an ogre, and she's obviously marrying within her species.

Just looking at Chelsea last night, it seemed she'd been marginalized by Fargo, made to feel less than she was. One thing in the world Wyatt did know was that Chelsea didn't deserve to be belittled by an ogre or the ogre's intended—to use fairy tale language. No wonder Chelsea had dropped the invitation when she extracted it from the envelope. The guy must have done her wrong. And Esther had been doing everyone wrong for years. Chelsea, however, took the brunt of it, from what Wyatt—and everyone else—had seen. Constant barrages of insults and scorn, like she thought of Chelsea as moldy, leftover fruitcake.

Maybe Chelsea still had some residual, unresolved feelings for the guy marrying her mean cousin.

Well, she'd better just pull herself together and get that dullard out of her system.

There was only one way Wyatt could think of to do that.

"Hey, Mack. Excuse me a second." Wyatt whipped out his phone and pulled up Chelsea in his contacts to text her.

Don't skip the wedding.

He hit send before he'd thought it through. What she needed was to take the best-looking, most successful man in Sugarplum Falls or the surrounding area. A message pinged back.

That's a change of tune. Why not?

Yeah. Good question. He tapped his temple a few times, as if the impact would shake loose a good idea. It shook loose an idea.

What do you want most if you go?

Mack cleared his throat. "I can come back if you're busy."

"Actually, that would be great." He shooed Mack out the door and then dialed Chelsea in a face-call. She appeared on the screen wearing that same ugly sweater from yesterday, and he asked, "What is your ideal outcome if you absolutely must go to that wedding?"

"Why this sudden interest in my ideal outcomes, Wyatt?" Chelsea had piled her long dark brown hair into a bun atop her head. Lately she'd been wearing it in that low ponytail that hugged the back of her neck and looked like a feral animal's tail. It wasn't really like her. Not the Chelsea she used to be.

"Inquiring minds want to know."

She aimed her gaze at the ceiling and then back at him. "I don't know. I mean, dream scenario? Which won't happen in a million years? That my ex takes one look at me and falls at my feet apologizing."

"Saying he made a big mistake letting you go. I get it." Wyatt nodded, picturing the moment with Fargo pretty much face down in the snow, kissing Chelsea's feet and blubbering. Yeah, that'd be a little bit of all right with Wyatt as well. "Okay. Well, here's a sound-bite for you: success is the best revenge."

"What does that even mean?"

"It means that if you have to go to the ogres' wedding, you shouldn't go alone."

"Ogres? What ogres?"

"Never mind. Just ... what you need is a date to the wedding with someone that will make both Fargo and Esther notice and who will fire up their jealousy."

Chelsea pushed her mouth to the side. "I don't know, Wyatt."

Oh, brother. If she was going to be difficult ... "Meet me at the bakery at five." If there was one thing he knew about himself it was that he was better at persuasion in person. "I'll buy."

"Can it be gingerbread?"

Yuck. Ginger. "Your choice. But you have to at least hear me out."

"Fine. I'll listen." The screen went dark.

Mack poked his head back in the door. "You done directing Chelsea Sutherland's social life and ready to talk about the Mom-Dad Investment Challenge yet?" He ho-ho-hoed at his own quip.

What had Mack been doing? Pacing outside Wyatt's office listening? That was so Mack.

"The team in accounting are having cake and said they'll wait until you can be there. The party don't start without Wyatt, they say." He flopped down in his usual chair."

"I'll have to skip it today. Can you check this out with me?" Wyatt looked a little closer at the file from Mom for a few minutes, with Mack making comments on the list of suggestions.

"It's a huge amount of money, you know." Mack pushed the file back toward Wyatt. "Like, ten percent of the bank's total investment fund."

Yeah. Wyatt rubbed the side of his head and groaned. This was the first thing he'd really, really wanted in a long time, and he could so easily fail. "If crunching numbers and calculating risk without regard to people or personalities is what it takes to make investments, I don't know, Mack. Is that really something I can do? You know me and my math skills. I'm much better at the human element. This is over my head." And above his pay grade. Maybe he should try to convince Mom and Dad to let him max out as a junior executive, not get promoted above his ability level. But then he'd never get to implement the much-needed adjustments to the company's direction.

North Star Capital used to be North Star Bank. When Mom had taken its helm from her daddy, she and Dad had reset its course—much too drastically. Somebody had to fix it, and Wyatt was the only one who could.

Except, could he?

"Don't look glum. You're an asset to the bank, Wyatt."

"I do know where my strengths lie, and where they don't." They lie with names and faces, with persuasion and enthusiasm, with building trust.

"Don't forget you have a business degree."

Only by the skin of his teeth. Those stats classes had ripped him to shreds. He'd focused on management, not finances—people, not hard numbers.

"Other than this part"—he waved a hand over the gaping black maw of the open file folder—"I'm confident that I could do a great job running this firm."

"Me, too. Everyone likes you. You know who's honest and who's not at a glance. You're a wizard with people. So, interview the people about these investments, and follow your gut."

But this wasn't about gut feelings. This was about cold, hard numbers. "Thanks for the vote of confidence." Wyatt shut the folder. "I'll do my due diligence." *Later.*

Mack turned to leave, but Wyatt called after him. "One last thing." Mack might know this, actually. "Can I ask you something in total confidence?" Probably not, since Mack liked a bit of gossip. But this might be his only avenue.

"Sure. Shoot."

"Have you ever heard any specifics on what makes my mom so dead-set against the Sutherland family?"

Mack's merry eyes lit up, and he smoothed his white shirt over his belly. "No, but I'd be more than happy to find out."

"Delicately, Mack."

"Of course. The woman's my boss. I'm not stupid."

There was that, for sure.

Mack left.

All afternoon, Wyatt dug into the backgrounds of the companies on the list—when his brain could focus on it. When he wasn't completely sidetracked by pondering the other problem he'd set himself up to solve today—one that might be much more delicate and with higher human stakes.

Five o'clock finally came, and Wyatt dashed out the bank's back doors and down Orchard Street to Sugarbabies Bakery. Chelsea was already at the counter, but he walked up beside her.

"Thanks again, Chelsea." Mrs. Toledo accepted her phone back from Chelsea's hand. "I would never have figured out how to change the default language back to English from Romanian without you. You're the best."

"No problem, Mrs. Toledo. It happens all the time. I'm everyone's go-to for tech and math needs. I'm used to it." She sounded slightly defeated. Probably because she hadn't eaten a cookie yet.

"Hello, Wyatt North." Mrs. Toledo flashed him a chubby smile.

"Merry Christmas, Mrs. T."

"It's merry now. I can't thank Chelsea enough."

"Me, neither. She's helped me with a few technical glitches in the past. Now, I'll take six gingerbread men," Wyatt said, "and a dozen of your famous strawberry jam thumbprint cookies." He pointed at the counter. "In separate bags, please, Mrs. Toledo."

"Ah, so the shortbread cookies with the hint of nutmeg won't get tainted by the ginger?" Chelsea asked under her breath while Mrs. Toledo filled the bags.

"Why else?" He handed Chelsea her sack of gingerbread men and they sat down in one of the comfy chairs placed in front of the wood-burning stove in the bakery's dining room. They both propped their feet on the ottoman between the chairs, and each pulled out a cookie.

Chelsea eyed her gingerbread man and chomped its left leg with an energy as if its name were Fargo Frye. "Thanks for the cookies. Very therapeutic." She bit off the other leg, and crumbs scattered on her lap. "I've been thinking about what you said, success is the best revenge, and I think you're right about firing up their jealousy, and I've been working on it."

"Oh? Working on it how?" Did she already find a date to the wedding? With …? A weird twinge went through him. "You found a date?"

Who? A long-latent spark of jealousy ignited.

"Sort of. I've been doing a lot of research, and there is an easy fix, and not very expensive, depending." She pulled her phone out and showed him the screen. "It's perfect. Stop looking at me like that. You're the one who said the words *fire up the jealousy*."

Inexpensive what? He leaned forward to see the screen. "Oh, no. Chelsea.

19

That … is not a good idea." In fact, it was a terrible idea. "You cannot *hire* a guy. Not like that, and definitely not from that site."

"Not all places are as disreputable as this site, per se. This just happened to be the most affordable."

Staring back at them from the *Firefighters by Day* website's portfolio were an array of muscular men wearing little more than fireman hats, their bedroom eyes, and seductive grins. Okay, to be fair, one guy did sport one of those white cotton tank-top shirts that signaled his penchant for domestic violence.

"What on earth are you thinking?" Wyatt plucked the phone from her hand and closed the site.

"Well, you said to make him jealous, and these were the best-looking guys I could find that I knew wouldn't turn down me or my credit card." She reached for the phone but missed. "There were some pretty smokin' guys there. I know Fargo and he'd be impressed. So would Esther. Jealous, even."

Probably true, but still. "Not happening." Absolutely not.

"Come on." She made one more grab for it, but he whisked it upward and out of her reach. "You didn't even let me show you the more expensive, less … *sketchy* sites. Think about it. I'd be helping someone earn a little money for the holidays. A service, really."

Service. Pah! "Forget that idea. Immediately." Her family wasn't populated by idiots. They'd discern in a second what was going on. Plus, Heath would kill her—and then kill Wyatt for letting it happen. "Immediately and forever."

Chelsea grimaced. "I don't really have any other options, Wyatt. In case you haven't noticed, this is the sound my radar makes when the date possibility scanner runs around the screen." She paused. "See? No blips. My dating field is completely empty, and I'm not on anyone else's radar either. Haven't been for ages." Chelsea folded her arms across her chest and harrumphed. "So, unless you have a better idea, *Firefighters By Day dot com* is what I'm doing."

Ha. Judging from the past, one of them would probably give her a discount if she promised to help him with his taxes. Cue the eye-roll for the girl who was always a guy's temporary math crutch. She pulled the sleeves of her ugly gray sweatshirt over her fingers.

"I do."

"Do what?"

"Have an idea."

"It'd better not be more expensive. I don't want to waste all my Christmas budget on—"

He held up his palm. "We'll think of someone local who will impress not only Fargo but also your family—because it's got to be someone better than he is." Not a tall order. "Then, you'll get the side-benefit of your family finding *him* more impressive than the groom."

"That would be a side-benefit, if it were even possible." Chelsea stuffed another cookie in her mouth. "Esther's side of the Sutherland family can't stop talking about how Fargo was so aptly named and is"—she affected a high, nasally voice—"probably going to 'live up to his name by *going far* in life.' I wish he'd go far, as in walk off the edge of the earth, but even that wouldn't be far enough."

Wow. What exactly had the guy done to wound Chelsea so much? "Then I'm right. And it has to be the right guy. Someone good-looking, employed, with a healthy dash of charm." Someone just like Wyatt. Did she see the flashing neon arrow pointing at him here?

"As if a guy like that existed, especially in Sugarplum Falls. And single? Ha. Ha-ha. See? I told you I'm blipless."

"That's just because you work from home and don't deal with the public as much as I do." Wyatt regularly saw which locals came in for investment advice, which ones came in asking for payday loans, and which ones came in to scheme ways to hide their income to avoid paying child support. She was right that most of them were not options. "There might be someone who's a perfect fit." *Me. Hello.* Other than the fact her immediate family might have a few qualms. But the point was to get under Fargo Frye's skin.

"Honestly, Wyatt, I'm dubious. There's a thing in math we term DNE: *Does not exist.* Like dividing a number by zero. Can't happen. Likewise, a guy like that in Sugarplum Falls? DNE."

"Maybe, maybe not." Probably not. But even a child-support dodger might be better than a hired-escort firefighter by day, fire-starter by night. "When will you see the happy couple?"

Chelsea looked alarmed. "It could be anytime. As soon as tonight."

"That doesn't leave me much time." If she wasn't going to accept the obvious choice—and with Heath's edicts still in force, how could she?—he'd better hunt up someone else. His mind scanned all his high school yearbooks, his client lists, the pews from church, the people on his weekend pickup basketball population. None. Not a soul. DNE. So, what other choice did he have? "If time is that tight, you're stuck with exactly one option."

"You're right. Give me back my phone and I'll sign up for a firefighter. I think the one who called himself *Coal* looked the least dangerous."

"Stop it, Chelsea. I'm talking about me."

Chapter 3

Chelsea

Wyatt! As her date for the wedding? But …

No one would believe it. No one would believe that she, Chelsea, could snag a guy like Wyatt. He was golden. The life of every party. And everyone knew it. Nobody as well as Chelsea did. He was the calm in the storm. He was the easy-going one who could make anyone smile. He was the guy who never met a stranger. Not to mention being North Star Capital's heir and basically Sugarplum Falls's most eligible bachelor other than maybe one of the Kingstons from the orchard.

Chelsea was none of those things. Not a soul would believe she could catch Wyatt's eye. Not in that way.

"You?" She lowered her voice and looked around Sugarbabies Bakery. Mrs. Toledo wasn't in sight, but that didn't mean she wasn't listening.

"Not just at the wedding proper. As your temporary boyfriend between now and the wedding festivities. It's not like you don't have to see everyone involved multiple times. Or have I misinterpreted Sutherland family get-together requirements?"

No, he'd probably even underestimated them. "Nobody has time for that, Wyatt. You have a job, a life." Sure, Wyatt had come to quite a few of her family events over the years, but he'd never been roped into every single mandatory Sutherland shindig. "I mean, I don't know when they'll start showing up. I've purposely *not* kept tabs on either of their lives."

Temporary boyfriend/girlfriend status with Wyatt? Really? Her mind was pinging like a pinball machine.

"Which means, they could be there as soon as tonight, like you said."

Chelsea closed her eyes. Tonight's event would be Sutherland-heavy. Everybody and their kids would be there for the hot cocoa preliminaries, where every Sutherland voted on the best flavor to use in the family's joint Hot Cocoa Festival booth.

She dragged out a sigh. "I'm so busy at work with that diabetes drug trial, I haven't even prepared a recipe." *Let alone prepped myself to come face to face with the last two people on earth I want to see.*

"Don't worry about that, I can probably come up with something on the fly."

No doubt about that. Wyatt could do anything. Charm anyone. He'd gotten every part-time job he'd ever applied for, and a few he hadn't applied for. He'd once talked two angry, sparring factions out of a brawl at a crowded hockey game. He'd been the single-most anticipated musical performance guest at the Sweet Haven Nursing Home every month. The elderly ladies just adored him.

Which probably meant that tonight, even when he winged it, everyone would probably be dazzled by his last-second concoction, and Chelsea and Wyatt would win *best cocoa*, and that alone would cement their status as a couple in the family's eyes.

You know what? No. "It's not going to work."

"Why not?"

For about ten huge and ten thousand small reasons. "For one, no sparks." At least on Wyatt's side. For Chelsea, there'd been a few glowing embers despite all the water Heath had thrown on that fire time and again. "We've been hanging out for years as friends, and to suddenly claim we're dating at the very *instant* my ex shows up with Esther? All the aunts will see through it." Not to mention Mom and Dad.

Oooh, or Heath, who may or may not show up tonight. And if not then, for sure at the Hot Cocoa Festival, where the cocoa powder wouldn't be the main thing in hot water.

"We can come up with something plausible. Stories about dating history don't have to be elaborate. How about, *things just clicked recently* or *it's been simmering a while*? Leave it at that."

No, the aunts would try to pry details out of her. "We'd have to settle on some finer points, though, just in case. You know my aunt Rita."

24

Wyatt sighed heavily. "So, what you're saying is that Coal, who will likely steal your wallet or your identity or worse, is preferable to me, Wyatt North, a guy you've known since you were the high school valedictorian."

Much longer than that, and no. Absolutely not what she meant. "It's not that. It's that ... Oh, I don't know."

Except she did know. If she did let herself pretend that they were dating, all that long-held-back interest in Wyatt could break through the dam. Of all the guys in her life right now—which, admittedly, was a small number at this point—only he had the potential to weasel his way into her damaged heart, seeing as how he already had a permanent address there, and put it in danger of being hurt much, much more.

In other words, only Wyatt had the ability to break her heart.

She wasn't ready for that. Not again. Not after what Fargo had done.

Geez, the jerk had even ruined math for her for a while and she'd taken zero joy in it.

"Sorry, but here's the bonging death-knell of that idea: what about Christmas Tree-O?" If they dated, it would get awkward after they broke up, and then the trio would crash land on the rocks. "Won't it be, I don't know, weird?"

"If we're fake dating? I don't know why."

Because then half the crowd won't show up, once they hear Wyatt is taken. And Chelsea would be on the receiving end of looks that had *nothing* to do with Christmas cheer.

"Have you even thought about how Heath would take it?" There. That was the true silver bullet to this ill-conceived plan. Which—while Chelsea appreciated the generous offer to sacrifice himself on the altar of preventing Chelsea's humiliation—could never work anyway, because no one in all of Sugarplum Falls would believe that Chelsea, as she stood today, could ignite a spark in any guy.

Especially a guy as charming and sought-after as Wyatt North.

Wyatt wadded the top of his cookie bag in his fist. "Heath won't like it, so I will grant you that."

Won't like it was putting it mildly. "I don't know who he'd kill first, you

25

or me."

Wyatt huffed a sigh. "Let's be honest, he'd kill that Coal dude first, if you showed up with him. Me, he'd torture slowly, then kill. He loves you. You're his sister."

Maybe, but Wyatt had been Heath's best friend since they were pre-teens having snowball fights, and Chelsea had been warned off. Multiple times. Apparently, in Heath's mind, Wyatt wasn't right for Chelsea and vice versa.

Just because Wyatt had dated a lot, did that mean he was no good for Chelsea, who'd dated almost no one seriously?

Wyatt stuffed his bag of cookies in the inner pocket of his coat. "Let's walk. We're going to be late for the hot cocoa tasting thing, and you need to get changed." He helped her to her feet. "Don't look at me like that. Your mom invited me last night when I was there picking up your mail."

Not a surprise. Mom had gotten used to Heath bringing Wyatt along to every Sutherland activity for a decade or more, and it was just habit now to expect him to be at family gatherings.

Chelsea dragged her snow boots as they trudged toward her car, which was parked beneath a lamppost tied with a huge red velvet bow. "It's ... we're either doing this or we're not doing this." And the clear decision should be *not.*

Except, did she have another option? There was no getting out of attending the wedding, and if she went alone, there was no attending with her self-worth intact. Esther would make sure of that, if the very sight of Fargo Frye didn't reduce Chelsea to ashes beneath the fire grate.

Which always stung. Chelsea and Esther had been ice skating pairs as little kids. They'd done matching Halloween costumes. They'd asked for matching dolls at Christmastime so they could play together.

But Esther's behavior since about age thirteen pretty much wiped all those times from memory. And her meanness to Chelsea in particular more than eclipsed any niceness that might have once resided in her.

Certainly, there was no one available in Sugarplum Falls who fit the better-than-Fargo bill better than Wyatt. He was successful, drop-dead handsome in a totally off-limits kind of way, and charismatic. If all the Sutherland aunts weren't decades his senior, they'd probably be swooning over him.

In fact, who was to say they weren't secretly?

Wyatt was right—it was too late to round up anyone else. *Unless ...* Unless Esther and Fargo weren't going to be there tonight. That would give her a little more time.

"So, is that a yes or a no?" Wyatt stood beside her at her car. A faint breeze stirred up both an eddy of powdery snowflakes at their feet, as well as bringing a faint hint of Wyatt's cologne to her senses.

Wyatt's cologne. *I'd better not start noticing that. Not now. Not ever.*

"Maybe they won't be there and the whole point is moot." She pulled out her phone. "I'll ask my mom."

Mom picked up. "Oh, honey, didn't I tell you? Tonight's cocoa-tasting is doubling as the family celebration engagement party for your cousin Esther and her fiancé." At least Mom had the kindness not to refer to him by name. She knew better. "Are you ... going to be okay with that? Esther has been pretty tough lately, but the real Esther is inside somewhere. Um, I know you and that young man have a history. It was months ago, so I thought maybe you'd dealt with it by now. If you want, we can ... Well, we really can't cancel or change it now. It's happening in about an hour."

"No, Mom. It's okay. Actually, I'll be bringing someone with me."

Mom was silent a moment, and then a burst of sound hit Chelsea's ear through the phone. "Someone, as in someone you're *seeing*?"

There was no going back now. She met Wyatt's gaze. He raised a single brow.

"It's new, Mom. So don't smother it, okay? Promise?"

"I'll be the soul of discretion."

Right. Chelsea would believe that when she saw it. Sutherlands and discretion didn't belong in the same sentence.

"My date is bringing our recipe submission." Take that, Wyatt. Of course, *take-thatting* him at this juncture wasn't cool. Plus, he'd cheerily volunteered to come up with something, so none of it had the least bit of punch.

Oh, blah.

"I can't wait to meet him, whoever he is. Don't be late if you want your

27

opinion on the cocoa flavor to count. You know the voting happens when it happens, and there's no leeway."

Chelsea hung up. Wyatt gave her that look again, the one halfway between a smoldering stare and an ironic sardonic moronic iconic, whatever. "What?" She chewed her lower lip. "Go ahead and say it."

"Nothing, nothing. Other than, I take it from that phone call, you've decided there's no time like the present, after all."

"If you count an hour from now as the present, then yes." Between now and then, Wyatt was right. Chelsea needed to get changed. Or, more like Chelsea had to make some kind of massive transformation. "Pick me up?"

"You know it."

She got in her car, and Wyatt swaggered down the sidewalk toward the bank where his car was parked.

What had she done?

Chapter 4

Wyatt

Wat had he done? After jogging back to his car, Wyatt sat in his SUV and gripped the wheel, watching his breath evaporate in the cold night air.

Heath was going to kick him out of the trio.

Well, maybe until Wyatt explained about Fargo and that *Coal* person and Chelsea's dire situation with regards to Fargo Frye. *What exactly was the situation?* He still didn't know details, but the direness was clear.

However, even with all those excuses—there'd always been crystal clear parameters Heath outlined for romantic relationships within Christmas Tree-O: *None.* Obviously those rules only applied to the big wall Heath built between Wyatt and Chelsea. The parameters had existed from the beginning when the three of them began singing together back when Heath and Wyatt were juniors in high school and Chelsea was a gawky eighth-grader so not on his radar that Wyatt had secretly rolled his eyes at Heath's mandate.

Of course, that eye-rolling had only lasted a few months, because soon Chelsea emerged from her middle-school gray-fuzz cocoon as a full monarch butterfly, gorgeous and poised and brilliant and irresistible with that alto voice and the way she moved when she sang.

That was when the older-brother threats had begun. *Touch her and die* was a famous one. *Think about her in a non-sisterly way and be neutered,* a classic. *Look at her like that one more time and don't plan on looking at anything ever again,* was probably the cherry on top.

Yeah, all of them had hit the clichés right on key.

Over the years, none of that changed, either. Not Wyatt's veiled interest or Heath's constantly clenched fist.

The truth was, Wyatt had made some immature moves as a teen while navigating the waters of dating and relationships. Besides, that, he wasn't good at math like Chelsea, or like his parents expected him to be in order to truly succeed in his career. He would never be good enough for Heath's sister. That was clear as any crystal bell ringing on Christmas morning. And probably not good enough for Ike and Iris Sutherland's daughter, either.

Ike had seen enough of Wyatt in the high school principal's office back in the day to have formed certain opinions, and Mrs. Sutherland, though warm as could be, might lose some of her warmth if she thought Wyatt's eye had fallen on their precious, brilliant daughter, especially from what she knew of Wyatt's dating past.

Yeah, he probably shouldn't have announced at a Sutherland family dinner that he'd accomplished his goal of dating and making out with every single one of the Sugarplum Falls High cheerleaders. Even Heath hadn't been impressed.

But if Heath had gotten out of the way and let me date who I was actually interested in, his sister, I wouldn't have had to keep trying to impress her for years and years. I wouldn't have turned into the flaky boyfriend they all knew me as. The guy who kissed and dissed girls who I thought of as placeholders.

All the Sutherlands liked him personally. For sure. However, there was no way they'd see him as a viable option for Chelsea. It was sort of Heath's fault. One percent. The lion's share of the fault was Wyatt's, and he knew it. He probably wasn't good enough for Chelsea, truthfully. But it didn't change the fact he wished he was.

Yeah, he'd better brace himself for family fallout, no matter who attended tonight.

Wyatt started his car and pulled out his phone to place an online order for takeout. Attending something like her ex's engagement party on an empty stomach was a terrible idea for Chelsea, who was probably some level of hypoglycemic. She definitely did her worst thinking on an empty stomach.

In fact, she'd probably been on a three-day fast when she started dating that Fargo Frye lecher.

Speaking of terrible ideas, so were the gray sweats she'd been wearing. Really, if she planned on making the type of impression she wanted, she'd better ditch them. Should he text and tell her?

Chelsea wasn't stupid. She'd know she needed to ditch those.

Right?

Lately, it seemed like she was smart about everything *except* her feelings. Walking it back through time, yeah. Sure enough, her transformation from Chelsea into … whatever image she was projecting these days coincided, time-wise, with getting her statistics degree and her job at the big pharma company.

For a while, Wyatt had assumed it was the plague of the work-from-homer: pajamas all day. However, now that he'd seen her reactions to Fargo and caught the tip of that iceberg, the Gray Sweats of Shame clearly had less to do with her working-from-home status and everything to do with the breakup that had occurred at the same time as her exit from Darlington State.

The jerk. If Wyatt were a fighter like Heath, running into that Fargo dude tonight could turn into a rematch of the Rumble in the Jungle, except at Holly Berry House. Which had a lot less menace in its title.

No, Wyatt couldn't fight the guy with fists. He'd have to find out exactly what Fargo Frye had done, and then concoct the perfect payback.

A tapping on his window startled him. He rolled it down to see Mack standing there shivering. "Your mom insists I hand you this." He shoved a long piece of paper through the window, like a grocery store receipt right before a long camping trip. On it were about a hundred names of women. "Here are the instructions. Look them over. Report back to her which you'll be taking out first."

"You can tell her I'll be taking out Chelsea Sutherland first." Whether or not she'd be a great *banking families alliance* candidate. Guh.

"Chelsea? As in, my cousin?"

"As in, yes."

"That's why you were asking about her this morning, isn't it? Do you have a death wish?"

"I'll handle Heath."

"I meant your mother."

Oh. "I'll let her know myself." Somehow. "Don't worry. I'm not throwing you under the bus."

31

"By the way, I did a little background research into that ... thing."

Wyatt's hands folded into fists. "Yeah?" The moment of truth.

"I won't disclose my sources"—he looked back and forth like he was both Woodward and Bernstein, and they were in a D.C. parking garage instead of a Sugarplum Falls bank's lot—"but she does have a lengthy history with Sutherlands from way back."

"As in?"

"Not clear on all details, and none of them seem like they could matter in isolation. But taken together, they make more sense. Look." He shoved another list through the window. "Remember, you didn't get this from me." Mack exhaled, steam forming in the cold air.

"You want to get in?" He aimed a thumb at the passenger seat. Wyatt wasn't ready to head into North Star just yet.

"Nah. Did you finish evaluating the list of recommended companies in the file?"

"No decisions yet. Any other insider info for me like the tip about Caldwell General Hospital?"

Mack looked back and forth again, as if someone in the North Star Capital parking lot might be listening. "Look deeper into ownership of all the companies before investing."

The list of suggested investments swirled in his mind. So many of them were businesses he'd never heard of in places Wyatt had never been.

"Good tip." North Star Bank had been a hometown firm, supporting local ventures, and if Wyatt could have some pull as a senior executive, it could be again, even though it had been renamed North Star Capital. "Here's my litmus test: unless something has local ties, it's off my short list."

Not that Mom and Dad wanted to see it as a chance to bolster the local economy. Stars were in their eyes for North Star.

He was out of time and would read Mack's list about Mom's history with the Sutherland family later.

Wyatt drove through Mario's and picked up manicotti with marinara. Mario's marinara made the world go round. *An opinion Chelsea and I share.* Maybe he should stop by the Sweetwater Boutique, too, and pick up something for her to wear. Chelsea absolutely couldn't show up to anything where Fargo might be while wearing those bad sweats or the nasty sweaters she'd been sporting for the past year or so.

Except, due to the sweatpants and shapeless oversized sweaters, there was no telling what size she might wear these days. He drove on past and didn't stop.

He turned in at Holly Berry House, followed the long gravel drive around the back of the main Sutherland residence, passing it toward Holly Berry Cottage where Chelsea lived.

"Knock, knock." He pushed the unlocked door open, like always. Christmas music was playing, and Chelsea was singing along to it. She had that rich, velvety voice he loved harmonizing with, and instinct made him hum along. "I brought Mario's. I hope that's okay." He held the *ay* a long time because in walked ... someone else. "Chelsea?" Wyatt blinked a few times, as if to clear the haze. "Is that you?"

In front of him hovered a ghost, as in a visitor from the past. There stood Chelsea Sutherland in a bathrobe, but her face aglow, her lips and cheeks a blush pink, her eyelashes dark fringes, and her indigo eyes sparkling.

Chelsea, it's you. The old Chelsea. Oh, and her hair wasn't matted to her head and then wadded up in that bunch at the back of her neck. It was styled in soft, raven curls and waves, like she'd just stepped out of the priciest, most upscale salon in Paris.

"You're looking at me like I'm a stranger."

Just the opposite. Like she was the long-lost girl of his dreams he used to drool over when her older brother wasn't looking. "I mean, you're not wearing your usual mathematician outfit."

"If I might run into Fargo Frye, I don't want him looking at me ... you know."

Right. But if she was going to run into anyone, they were going to look. And keep looking. And have a hard time tearing their eyes away.

"You're not planning on the bathrobe, though. Obviously." Not that Wyatt minded the short thing that showcased her long legs, but still.

"That's where I'm stuck. My wardrobe isn't exactly show-stopping." She smushed her lips into a frown. "You brought Mario's? Did I hear the magic word marinara?"

"And breadsticks." He put the bags on the table and retrieved Christmas-themed dinner plates and utensils from the kitchen while Chelsea wafted the scent of the Italian culinary masterpiece from the bag to her nose. "You do know that my mom taught Mario in high school culinary classes, right?"

"She did?" Wyatt put the plates down and joined her at the table with the evergreen boughs and candle with the plaid ribbon as centerpiece. They dished out the manicotti, said grace, and then dug in. "She must be pretty proud of that."

Wyatt had provided a behind-the-scenes loan to keep Mario's afloat a couple of years ago after the restaurant's roof blew off in a storm when their insurance hadn't covered it. Mom and Dad hadn't been aware of the transaction. No one but Wyatt and Mario knew. It had been repaid in full, but even now, Mario always made sure Wyatt received extra breadsticks.

"I don't know if proud is the right word, but happy for Mario." Chelsea took a bite and closed her eyes. "This is … mmm. How he balances the tomato with the oregano and garlic in such perfection, I'll never know, but I love it."

Wyatt kept staring at Chelsea's mouth as she chewed. Her full lips were so much fuller today, more accentuated, more … tempting.

No. He wasn't tempted, even if they started fake-dating. Fake-dating couldn't include any kissing. Not if word of this so-called relationship could get back to Heath.

But those lips, that mouth, the soft curve of her face. How could he have been blind to it for so many months? Years?

Because Heath had put blinders on Wyatt, that's how. And he'd super-glued them on.

They talked about the upcoming events—the Waterfall Lights concert, the town Christmas play, the Hot Cocoa Festival that loomed this very weekend. They decided that Heath had better not stand them up with his whole *try to be there* attitude. Christmas Tree-O was a *trio* by definition, and they didn't have any duets prepared in case he ditched them for yet another *work commitment*. As if Chelsea and Wyatt didn't have work commitments.

"Oh!" Chelsea startled as a blop of marinara landed on the lapel of her white fluffy robe, just at the curve of her chest, which—was it more ample than before? "It's a good thing I wasn't dressed yet."

Not dressed. Not dressed. *I mean, she's dressed. Covered. Clothed. There's no difference between the clothed-ness of wearing a robe and wearing, say, a wrap dress.* Except for some reason, in this moment, there was.

"Let me help." He leaped up, grabbed a dish cloth and wet it at the sink. Then he hustled back to her side, where he gently daubed the spill.

The knuckle of his index finger faintly grazed her collar bone, and he froze.

Since when is Chelsea's skin soft as the down of a thistle?

"You're being extra solicitous. Is that a perk of being your temporary girlfriend?" She took the cloth from him and set it aside. As she did so, the sides of their hands brushed, and suddenly Wyatt became highly aware of the skin on the side of his hand. Because it had lit on fire.

"Uh, of course." He swallowed hard and sat back down at his meal. His stomach was too full of something else, something doing a holiday polka, to fit even another bite, even of Mario's. "Better throw that robe in the wash quick or the sauce will stain it." Like an idiot, he stared to see whether she'd obey immediately.

She did not.

"Now that I've ruined wardrobe Plan A"—she cleared her dish and headed toward her bedroom—"the bathrobe look is out. I'm going to have to figure out plan B. What's left is stretched out sweaters and gray sweats."

"No gray sweats." Or stretched out sweaters. "You sure you don't have something else?"

He should have stopped by Sweetwater Boutique.

Wyatt followed her into the walk-in closet. The space was tight, but at this proximity, he could breathe in her hair products and whatever floral soap she'd used. "What's back here?"

"Not sure. I just shoved my stuff at the front and pushed Grandma's items to the back."

Wyatt riffled through the hangers. "What about this one?" He tugged out a 1950s style dress in the same indigo as Chelsea's eyes. "Are you her size?"

"From when I knew her, she wasn't this size." Chelsea looked it over. "This is actually pretty nice. I like the shirt-waist and the full skirt." Wyatt held it up to her. "Okay, I'll try it on. Grandma wouldn't mind, would she?"

"Nope." Grandma Sutherland had been gone a few years and wouldn't mind.

Wyatt left the room, and went to sit at the piano while Chelsea changed. They were already a few minutes late for the cocoa event at the house, but for some reason he didn't regret a single minute of disappointing Mrs. Sutherland over his punctuality. *She knows me well enough to know my skills in that area. Or lack thereof.*

He played a few bars of the recent radio hit "Christmas Kissing." Uh, no. Wrong. No going there. No matter how good she'd looked tonight.

In self-preservation, he fled the piano and sat down at their Scrabble game. What could he do with the letters *S-I-S-K-E-R-H*? Sheiks? But that didn't use all the letters to get him the bonus. To stay ahead of Chelsea's score, Wyatt needed all the bonuses he could get.

On the little wooden rack he arranged and rearranged them. H first, S first, R first, K first ...

KISS HER.

Oh, great. Now even the Scrabble game was conspiring against him, like everything else. *It's like the universe wants me to fall for Chelsea.*

"How do I look?" Chelsea stepped out of the bedroom, twirled, and then pressed the skirt back down after it flared during the spin. "Is it too ...?"

Nuh-uh. It wasn't *too* anything. Except too alluring. With his tongue thick in his mouth and most of his muscles limp, he started rambling. "Dressmakers in the fifties sure knew how to make a woman's body look feminine."

The indigo dress tapered in a tight *V* from her shoulder to her waist, which was so narrow it almost looked improbable. Then, it flared out at the hips. He'd better not even note how well it accentuated Chelsea's surprisingly full chest with its sweetheart neckline coming to a point at a series of tightly-spaced buttons down her front.

"Sorry for being so slow. It took forever to button." She fingered the

36

buttons at the top. "I guess it's a little snug. I'm bubbling out at the top here a bit. Is it indecent? Should I change?"

No. No, siree. "There's not really time." Was that a good tangential excuse? "I don't want your mom to think I'm standing her up. She did invite me."

The side of Wyatt's hand began to burn again, like it had when they'd touched earlier. That thing Chelsea had said about *no sparks*? It was dead wrong.

Chapter 5

Chelsea

Even though it was steps through the snow to Holly Berry House, Wyatt insisted they drive together in his car. "You don't want your grandma's shoes to get ruined in snow."

Granted, the vintage high-heels should be babied.

Wyatt jumped out of the car at Holly Berry House and got her door, and then he held her by the arm to lead her up the front steps, past the million Christmas lights Dad had hung and through the wreath-bedecked door and into the house.

Inside, every breath was laced with warm chocolate, plus there was a hint of the scent of wood burning in the fireplace. Loud conversations rose over piped-in Christmas music, and squeals of little kids filled the airwaves.

Home. It smelled and felt and sounded like home.

The only thing not ringing true in this picture was Wyatt. Not that *he* was out of place. In fact, he probably spent more time in Holly Berry House these days than Chelsea did, more or less hanging out with Ike and shooting the breeze on random topics from religion to politics to the hockey season's prospects. No, it was the *Chelsea and Wyatt* combo that jarred her sensibilities. It made her cling more tightly to his arm, just to keep steady.

And a very sturdy arm it was, which she needed a lot in Grandma's spectator pumps to keep herself from falling down. If Grandma's dress was snug, then these shoes were positively pinchy. But it wasn't like Chelsea could have worn her foam snow boots with the dress or her Birkenstock sandals, which were her only two footwear choices at this point.

She stepped onto the wood floors, and a puddle of melted snow made her slick shoe-bottom slide, pulling her leg forward and nearly putting her into a gymnast's splits.

"Yikes!" She clutched Wyatt's arm, unable to catch her full breath in this tight bodice. "Wyatt!"

But Wyatt didn't let her down. Literally. He flexed his arm, keeping her upright, and then lifted her back to her unsteady feet. "You all right?"

Whew. "Good save."

"Welcome home, kids!" Dad interrupted the accidental hug and added one of his own. "Great to see you here tonight. Wyatt, anytime you're in my home, I'm happy."

"Better than in your office, eh?" Wyatt and Dad always shared this banter, every time he showed up for a Sutherland family event or community service project.

"No pranks tonight, young man."

"Just one teeny one?"

"All right. One. But keep it clean."

"You got it."

"Right. Now, I'm busy with the proceedings, but get yourselves to the kitchen and drink some cocoa." He pinched Chelsea's cheek and said, "Mom said you're bringing a date. Good. Good!" He grinned wide and left.

Wince. Chelsea should have explained that Wyatt was the date, but Dad left too quickly.

They made their way through the chaos, dodging a small dog racing through the room, a baby learning to walk, and the piano bench which was being used as a blanket fort. Finally, they stepped over what sounded like a violent game of Candy Land raging between her cousin Mack's children.

"You can't just choose any card you want from the stack, Kaden." Jaidyn pounded her hand on the board, toppling all the little gingerbread men. "That's cheating."

Instead of defending himself from his little sister's accusations, Kaden looked up.

"Uncle Wyatt! You're here!" He jumped up and threw his arms around Wyatt's legs. "Finally. We heard you were making the gross-out flavors of hot cocoa, so we were saving up room." Kaden patted his belly.

"I am."

He was? "You are? What does that even mean?" And since when had he become *Uncle* Wyatt? "Please say you're not adding mustard. Or anchovies."

"Who's that lady?" Kaden asked. "She looks all red in the face."

"Hey, buddy." Wyatt scrubbed the top of Kaden's head. "Good to see you. Merry Christmas, Kaden. You winning the game?"

"No. Yes. Merry Christmas." The Sutherland kid, with his Sutherland signature nose, narrowed his eyes on Chelsea. "I have seen you somewhere before. Are you on TV or something?"

"Kaden." Chelsea was going to have to put a stop to this. "Knock it off. You know me."

Rubbing his eyes, Kaden took a step backward, kicking the game board, ruining what was left of their game. "Aunt Chelsea?"

Technically, no. She was not his aunt. She was his mom's first cousin. But the Sutherland family did extend aunt status broadly. "Merry Christmas," she said. "You ready for the cocoa voting?"

"You look ... *totally* different." Kaden was staring openly at her chest, bless his seven-year-old brazenness.

Her kingdom for an infinity scarf right now. What had she been thinking, showing off this much of her assets?

"*Really* different," Kaden went on. "I thought for a second you were from that new Barbie doll movie that Jaidyn likes watching. She's always watching Barbie movies, and you look just like Barbie's friend with the dark brown hair." He turned around. "Doesn't she, Jaidyn?"

Jaidyn came running, and confirmed. "Yeah, like Raven." But she wasn't as impressed or thrown for a loop. Instead she asked Wyatt, "What kind of cocoa are you making for us? You better hurry. Our dad said it's almost over."

Were they really that late?

Wyatt breezed it off. "You'll see. We're calling it Caliente Cocoa." He waved goodbye to the kids and led Chelsea into the kitchen, sliding his fingertips down her bare arm and placing his palm against hers. He looped just his index fingertip through hers, linking them together. "I know *caliente* means temperature hot, not spicy hot, but can we just go with it?"

They were in the kitchen now, and the steaming pot of hot cocoa base rested on the stove. He dipped in and pulled out a few ladles of it. None of the rest of the family was at hand, so Chelsea exhaled. No need to make up excuses or stories about their dating.

Yet.

"Can I help?" Chelsea asked, settling herself on a bar stool at the huge kitchen island.

The adults were making a ruckus in the living room area near the fireplace, and empty Styrofoam cups littered the countertops, toppled here and there beside a variety of labeled pitchers: *Salted Caramel Marshmallow Cocoa, Lavender Mint Cocoa, Bitter Orange Cocoa, Raspberry Brownie Fudge Cocoa, Rhubarb Cocoa.* Lots more. This was going to be a good year and hard to judge.

"You said I was in charge of our entry. You sit back and relax."

"Can I at least pour you a taster's cup of any of these?"

"Sure." Wyatt was in the fridge and pulled out a small red bottle. "I'm almost done."

Chelsea took a few fresh white cups from the top of the stack and poured two of each flavor, readying them for taste-testing. "Are you thinking of entering yours? We might be too late, since it looks like ballots are collected, and there's a lot of noise in the other room."

"Nah, I'm only doing this for the kids. Do you really think the adults would want to taste *this?*" He held up a pitcher half-full of cocoa in one hand and a bottle of Tabasco sauce in the other. "Do you think five shakes is enough?"

"I don't know. Let me taste and see."

"Seriously?" Wyatt froze, which indicated he'd really meant it when he'd promised Dad a small prank.

"Sure." Chelsea had better taste it to see whether it was going to be so hot it garnered tongue lashings from the moms. "Just a sip." She took the cup from his hand. Did he purposely touch her fingers? She pressed it to her mouth, tasting the steaming liquid. "Ooh! It has an after-bite." She pushed it back at him.

Wyatt took the cup, twisting it. Why? He lifted it to his mouth, watching her over the rim with his dark eyes. "Just right." He set the cup down, and then shook his head quickly. "You're right about the bite." He lifted it again—oh. And drank from the place where her lipstick stained the cup.

Chelsea's spine stiffened. Was he *flirting* with her? Touching his mouth to the space her mouth had touched?

"Wyatt—" What? What did she want to say, that he didn't need to flirt with her, that it wasn't a necessary part of the bargain, and that he didn't actually need to try? Or that he definitely *shouldn't* try? Please, just to save her from getting too caught up in the ruse? "I poured us both some cocoa. Should we taste them all?"

He came around and took the first cup. Wyatt affected a sober stance and tone. "A lot is riding on this. We must take this seriously."

"Wyatt."

"No, Chelsea. It matters which flavor combination the Sutherland family presents to the town of Sugarplum Falls at this year's Hot Cocoa Festival, you know. It's not like the public won't be expecting the pinnacle of flavor from the family. We can't let them down by voting irresponsibly."

"All right then." Chelsea tasted the salted caramel marshmallow first. "What do you think?"

They went down the whole lineup of steaming cups, with Wyatt making comments like, *full-bodied flavor* and *floral after-effects.*

"I think I'm ready to make my decision." Wyatt set down the final cup. "And I don't take this task lightly." He reached for a ballot from the stack on the end of the counter. "Are you prepared to do your bounden duty, my love?"

His love. "Um ..." She accepted the ballot, but his term of endearment echoed too loudly in her head to allow for complex thought to break through.

"Who is whose love?" Mom rounded the corner. "Wyatt! I didn't hear you come in. And who is ... Chelsea?" Mom skidded to a halt in her near-hug of Wyatt. "Chelsea, are you wearing Grandma's dress?"

"Um." Seemed that she only had faculties enough to create that single syllable.

"Doesn't she look great in it?" Wyatt put an arm around Chelsea's shoulder and tugged her to his side. In these shoes, she fit perfectly beneath his arm, like they'd been carved from the same block of wood. He squeezed her shoulder and excused himself. "I'll be back in a minute." He headed down the hallway toward where the washroom lay.

Mom whirled on her. "Chelsea, honey. I thought you were going to bring the person you're seeing." She looked after Wyatt. "Did your date fall through?"

"Um ..."

"I'm glad Wyatt made it. He told me he would make special cocoa for the kids, and I shouldn't have announced it to Mary's kids, Kaden and Jaidyn, since you know Wyatt. He's not always a hundred percent reliable."

He wasn't? Perpetually late, yes. And that would bug Mom.

Mom took a cleansing breath. "I must say, your date should be eating his heart out for standing you up tonight. You look stunning in Grandma's dress. I remember she wore that the day Grandpa received his flight orders to go to Korea. She kissed him goodbye on the runway. I'll show you the picture sometime. You make it look even better than she did, I must admit. You're more ... well-endowed. In fact, you should highlight that fact more often, you'll get a few more dates, even here in Sugarplum Falls. There might be a few nice divorcés in your age range whose head you could turn if you dressed like this a little more often. Signaled your interest in dating."

"Um ..." What on earth could she say to that?

"I did happen to tell a few of your aunts that you'd be bringing someone tonight, which was a mistake, I know now. I should have waited until—"

Wyatt swept into the room. He stalked toward Chelsea, his eyes boring into hers. "Sorry I was gone so long. The kids are coming to get their cocoa." He took her in his arms, tugging her close, his warmth enfolding her and causing every sector of her nervous system to go into Wacky Mode, unable to even loosen her stiff arms pinned at her side as he pulled her into his torso. "But you're right, Mrs. Sutherland. Chelsea has the power to turn heads. Always has, at least mine." He pressed his lips softly to her temple. It might have left a burn mark.

"Chelsea?" Mom sounded alarmed. "Just ... wait. Hold on a second here."

A croak formed at the back of Chelsea's throat, and try as she might, it wouldn't swallow down. She met Mom's eyes around Wyatt's shoulder. Mom looked like she'd just been shown the North Pole and that Santa really *did* have a workshop and elves and a flying sleigh.

"It's *Wyatt* you're seeing?" she said, her voice hoarse and nothing short of *sore amazed*. "You two? You're dating Wyatt North?"

With fierce effort, Chelsea moved her head up and down a fraction of a centimeter. "Uh-huh," she said weakly. Oh, they were going to be called on the carpet for this ruse.

"I guess shocked isn't the word for it, exactly."

Oh, dear. Was Mom against it? She had said Wyatt wasn't reliable. Beyond a complete lack of punctuality, there had to be something more to her obvious disapproval. Sure, he'd spent quite a bit of time in Dad's principal's office for pranks. But none of them had been harmful pranks. At least none Chelsea knew of. Was it the fact he'd dated around a little? Make that a lot. And there had been that whole cheerleader makeout conquest thing. Yeah, and the time he'd forced Heath to switch dates with him at the prom because he'd decided Heath's date was prettier. Or something along those lines, but she couldn't recall exactly.

Yeah, Mom really might not be impressed by those choices.

Unreliable as a loyal boyfriend must be what she meant.

Luckily, he was only a fake boyfriend, so it didn't matter. Not that she could explain it to Mom that way.

But his hug sure felt reliable. She sank into it a little more and inhaled his cologne.

"Mrs. Sutherland." Wyatt released Chelsea and turned to face Mom. Before he could finish, and before Chelsea could come up with anything to say, into the kitchen strode Aunt Lisa.

"Merry Christmas!" The woman had presence. No wonder she was the town's mayor for a third term.

"Merry Christmas, Mayor Lang." Wyatt, for one, could speak. He turned on his charm. "Don't you look nice in red."

"Don't you look handsome in everything, Wyatt North. Well, hello,

44

niece." She turned toward Chelsea, her gaze darting to the manly, possessive arm draped around Chelsea's shoulders. In her loudest mayoral voice she boomed, "Well, lah-di-dah and do-re-mi. I heard you were bringing a beau tonight, Chelsea, dear. This is just amazing." She wiped her forehead. "I'm so glad we get *some* romance tonight, since my own daughter and her fiancé didn't deign to show up for their own engagement party."

No Fargo and Esther? Really? *I got all dressed up for nothing.* But then, her eyes flicked toward Wyatt, and he was giving her another once-over. Maybe not for nothing. Could it be termed a *once* over if it had happened a dozen or more times?

Wyatt's gaze had weight. Tangible heft. There might be a mathematical equation for it.

"Before you two go into the living room and join the party, tell me, how did this"—Mom waved her hand between the two of them—"start?"

"Yes. You've supposedly been nothing but friends for years." Aunt Lisa tapped her foot and crossed her arms. "What changed? Or were you hiding it all along? If so, you're as good of an actress as your cousin Paris! Who, by the way, *didn't* get the role of Caroline in the town Christmas play this year—to everyone's shock. But I digress. What I'm saying, is you've been holding out on us."

Chelsea's ears pounded. Shoot! All day Chelsea had reminded herself to come up with a plausible catalyst, but nothing had stuck. And the truth was too embarrassing. No way was she telling Mom it was a ruse to make Fargo apologize.

Her mind scampered from idea to idea, and she seized on one at last: "Freak mistletoe accident."

Aunt Lisa burst into laughter. "The chemistry finally clicked when your lips locked! I love it. It's the stuff romance novels are made of." She bellowed more laughter. "Lucky you, and just in time, too. I was about to pounce on Wyatt here to put his name in the matchmaking blind-date-setup Santa hat at the Hot Cocoa Festival tomorrow night. Skin of your teeth, eh, young man?" She held up her hand for a high-five, which he responded to with a loud smack and an *aw yeah.*

Look at him! Just reveling in it! Chelsea had to forcibly close her mouth from gaping.

"Okay, then. Let's see it." Aunt Lisa tapped her invisible watch. "I've got cocoa results to hear so no time to dilly-dally. Get going."

"Going where?" Chelsea asked.

"Get going on the instant replay. You know you're not getting off that easily. You know how I love a good budding romance."

"Lisa, I don't think—" Mom to the rescue. Bless her for remembering Chelsea's *don't smother it* plea.

"Of course they want to repeat it."

"Maybe not in front of *us,* though." Mom steered Aunt Lisa by the shoulders. Few could manage such a feat with the town mayor. "Sorry, Chelsea. I can't take her anywhere."

"I'll be back," Aunt Lisa hollered over her shoulder. "Don't think you're getting off this easily."

Chelsea fell back against the kitchen island's counter. "That was a close one."

"What, that you don't have to see Fargo and Esther?"

That, too. She stared up at Wyatt, suddenly noticing how soft and inviting his lips looked. *I haven't given them a good stare in a while.*

"I'm sorry, what did you say?" Chelsea blinked herself back into the moment. "I missed the question." *Because I was studying the contour of your upper lip, thinking how it would feel pressed against mine.* Oh, it had been far too long since she'd been kissed.

Ew, and the last time had been Fargo. And before that, only a few weird guys her college freshman year, though they'd given her a little practice so she wasn't embarrassingly bad at it. So, bless them and their weirdness.

"I said, are you relieved or disappointed?" Wyatt bumped her shoulder. "But why are you looking like you've tasted rotten eggnog all of a sudden?"

No sense telling him about kissing Fargo. "Let's just go into the living room and join the party. They'll be announcing the cocoa winners any second now. I'm pulling for the salted caramel marshmallow."

They went in, where Dad had the crowd gathered and rapt. He was using

46

his old standby *principal in the auditorium* voice. Stentorian was his word for it.

"The winners of this year's cocoa voting are Rita and Lester! Their Raspberry Brownie Fudge Cocoa squeaked out ahead of the caramel-marshmallow flavor. Next year, Jolene. Next year."

Aunt Jolene gave a resigned shrug. It was hard to beat Rita's flavor combinations, and everyone knew it. "Congratulations to the winners."

Everyone clapped.

Wyatt turned to Chelsea. "What? You voted for marshmallow? Not the Caliente Cocoa by yours truly?"

"It wasn't even in the voting." She paused and looked up at him and turned on her sweetest flirtatious voice. "Don't worry, Wyatt. *You* always have my vote." She gave a funny little sigh.

Flirting was not her forte.

"Don't do that, Chelsea."

"Do what?"

"Make me think you mean it." Wyatt frowned. "I'd better go."

Chapter 6

Wyatt

Wyatt stood at Chelsea's side next to the stage at the Sugarplum Falls recreation center, ten minutes before Christmas Tree-O's set performance time. The whole ceiling had been draped with dark fabric, and little Christmas lights pierced the darkness, creating the effect that they were all outside on a cold winter's night for this town festival.

Good job, town council and chamber of commerce. Wyatt probably would have shown up for one of the meetings to help as a rep from North Star Capital, but Mom didn't really go in for that stuff.

Maybe that's why she despises the Sutherlands. They make her look bad by comparison with all their volunteering.

"It smells like chocolate and peppermint in here." Chelsea didn't look the least bit nervous. Like always. But Wyatt's stomach was busy with gymnastics auditions.

"Watch out." He pulled her to his side before she got pummeled by someone's stray child with a sticky peppermint candy. Kids ran everywhere, and the booths around the edges of the room featured hot chocolate and decorated Christmas trees, while the center area featured Christmas-themed carnival games like Pin the Nose on Rudolph.

"Thanks. Wow, everyone's here."

The whole town had seemingly turned out to swill warm, multi-flavored cocoa and mill around to holiday music to get into the Christmas spirit. Even that stoic bookstore-owning widower Sam Bartlett was here.

"Not quite everyone is here, though." He scanned the Hot Cocoa Festival crowd. "No Heath."

Which put a severe damper on the festiveness of the night. Why hadn't he showed up?

"Can we wing it?" Chelsea hugged herself—and this time not from the comfort of one of those shapeless sweaters. Instead, she'd found a dark purple silk blouse that had a sheen that brought out the violet in her indigo eyes and set off her dark brown hair, making it almost shimmer. Plus, her legs stemming up from those killer heels? A man could be put on the naughty list just for noticing them—and on the blind list for not.

"Wing it?" Uh, maybe. "What if we just sing our parts? Maybe no one will notice."

"That there isn't a melody?" She tugged at the ends of her hair. Maybe she was, actually, a little off-balance. "You should have come over this morning. Or stayed later after the family thing last night. We should have practiced or come up with some sort of contingency plan." She lowered her voice. "Or at least come up with a better story. With more details. That mistletoe accident thing was weak."

True on all counts. "It's too late now." Some girl in the crowd kept waving to him and winking flirtatiously, mouthing call me. "Maybe Heath will still show and it won't matter."

"Why did you leave early last night?" Her stare penetrated him, those indigo eyes soft and imploring. Hard to resist. "You didn't even walk me home last night."

Ah, that. It was complicated. No way did he want to get into it right now, not when they had a full-on Christmas Tree-O emergency pressing in on them. And even after the emergency passed, he might not want to relive the emotions tied to Mrs. Sutherland's disapproving reaction to finding out that Wyatt was dating her daughter.

You two? You're dating Wyatt North?

The sting had reached deep inside him, and had festered the longer he stayed at Holly Berry House. Always Mrs. Sutherland had been so accepting of Wyatt, making him feel like one of her own. Now, I'm dating Chelsea and all of that changes? It had been almost worse than he'd foreseen.

It wasn't normal, he knew, to feel more rejection from his girlfriend's mother than from the girl herself. But such was the case.

I thought I was her favorite. "I'll answer that question if you answer mine." He turned her away from the crowd, toward the hot cocoa booths again, away from the view of the Sutherland family entry with Aunt Rita's winning Raspberry Brownie Fudge Cocoa. "Why didn't you take your aunt Lisa up on her request to show her how we kiss under the mistletoe?"

"Wyatt!" Chelsea stiffened. "Shush."

A little boy careened into Chelsea's legs, grabbing her by the striped tights. "Help! She's going to hit me!" He buried his face in Chelsea's skirt.

"Who's going to hit you?" Chelsea patted his back. Was something terrible going on at the Hot Cocoa Festival? She glanced around for someone looking angry.

Instead, she saw a little girl with a candy cane-striped pool noodle, curved at the end.

"I found you!" She skidded to a halt, looking up at Chelsea. "You're very pretty for an elf." She took on a mature heir. "I'm Adele. Will you help me whack my brother Mac? He sniffed in my root beer."

"Sniffed in your root beer?" Chelsea crouched down to look in the little boy's eyes. He had to be about six, and the sister looked to be eight. "Did you sniff in Adele's root beer, Mac?"

Mac nodded. "And she's going to hit you."

Up walked their dad. "Kids?" He took both their hands, pulling them to his side. "Sorry, Chelsea. Hi, Wyatt. These two escaped." Beau Cabot wiped his forehead. He looked spent. "I can command all the troops in my Air Force Reserve unit any weekend or military exercise you ask, or kick trash in the board room of Tazewell Solutions, but put me in charge of two fighting kids, and I'm just managing chaos."

"Good to see you, Beau." Wyatt patted the single dad's shoulder. "You're doing great with them. Plus, this is a kid-friendly event. No worries."

"Besides, your daughter called me a beautiful elf, so she's won my heart forever." Chelsea smiled down at Adele. "Right? Besties?"

Adele grinned, showing missing teeth, and Beau whisked them off to play the Christmas version of the carnival game whack-a-mole. Which he seems to feel like he's playing all day with those kids.

Wyatt lowered his voice. "He's holding up, right?"

A deep breath, and Chelsea shrugged. "I keep thinking his wife will change her mind. He needs help with those kids—and not just babysitters. He needs a partner to raise them."

"Hey, guys." Up walked Poppy Peters, owner of the Cider Press beverage shop, and curtailed the conversation about Beau Cabot before Wyatt responded. "Are you singing together or are you, as rumors say, together together?"

Chelsea stiffened. Wow. Sugarplum Falls should advertise itself as being a housing location exclusively for people who didn't like to beat around the bush.

"We're dating." Chelsea pulled a tight smile and lifted a shoulder. "It's new."

Fortunately, Poppy got distracted when Mayor Lang called for her to come to the blind-date-setup hat event. "Sorry, gotta go. Mayor Lang knows how to keep me at her beck and call."

"That I believe." Wyatt grimaced in empathy.

Poppy trudged off toward her blind date doom and that Santa Hat matchmaker thing.

"Sorry about Aunt Lisa's tactlessness last night. She's just pushy. You've been in Sugarplum Falls long enough to know what a character she is."

"That wasn't the question. You haven't answered the question." The kiss reenactment question.

Mayor Lang's voice came over the PA system. "We've got our soon-to-be couples lined up. Is everyone ready for the blind-date setups? The hat doesn't make a mistake." She laughed into the microphone too loudly and it screeched. Flanking Mayor Lang were a row of men on one side and a row of women on the other. Ah, her victims, all wearing deer-in-the-headlights stares.

Poor saps.

Wyatt should thank Chelsea for saving him from that fate, if nothing else. Even if he wasn't really good enough to be her *real* date, according to her mom and brother.

What would a guy have to do to get them to take him seriously?

51

"I know, I know. You all read the order of events for tonight and were expecting a performance by town treasure Christmas Tree-O, but my nephew Heath is M.I.A."

A rumble went through the crowd. Stinking Heath. Wyatt's stomach did a triple backflip.

"The good news is a little bird tells me the remaining duo of the Christmas Tree-O might have a romantic song ready for us to hear." She clapped until the audience did too. "While we put the final touches on the hat event, please welcome Chelsea Sutherland and Wyatt North. Christmas *Duo*. Come on up here, you two."

Uhhhhh. He gripped her hand. "What romantic song?"

Over the speakers came the unmistakable introductory notes of the most notorious and controversial Christmas duet there ever was: "Baby, It's Cold Outside."

Ugh. There was no escaping it, no matter *how* much it made everyone's skin crawl—luckily, they'd altered the *what's in this drink?* lyrics a while back to dial down the not-so-savory overtones. The crowd would get those tonight.

"Wyatt, we can skip it if you're not feeling it. This song is terrible."

"Nope." He was feeling a lot of things, but not like skipping a semi-romantic song with Chelsea. It might be his only chance. Wyatt took her hand. "You know there's no arguing with that mayor. Let's give them what they came for."

They arrived at the microphones on the stage in time for Chelsea to sing the opening line, insisting she really couldn't stay.

Wyatt grabbed his mic, telling Chelsea she should, in fact, stay, due to the temperature. He grabbed her hand and kissed the back of it, which the crowd loved, and Chelsea reacted with perfect alarm—drawing laughs.

Luckily, he didn't take her too off guard. She made it for her lines, which insisted she needed to leave. Wyatt's lyrics argued again, the chill his main point. He slipped an arm around her waist, tugging her close.

She was resisting, but he kept insisting. It went back and forth, with her tugging away, and Wyatt tugging her back. Wyatt called her beautiful, as the lyrics required, and told her not to hurry. Chelsea reacted, her face blushing, talking about her maiden aunt's worry. The audience started to laugh, getting into it.

Wyatt pulled her into dance hold, spinning her a couple of times. It was working, they were charming the audience.

At the chorus's harmony, he took the melody and Chelsea harmonized. It was as if they'd practiced—they just fell into it naturally, the chemistry between them crackling, despite the lame lyrics. He looked down into her eyes, and they were wide, warm, inviting. *I could stare into them for hours. It's like gazing at the moon on a dark night.*

They hit the final note, and the bass drum accompaniment signaled the end, but their eyes were still locked. Chelsea's cheeks were flushed, and she was just inches from his face.

I could kiss her now.

The audience gave its approval with applause. A couple of wolf whistles shrilled. One smart aleck shouted, "Kiss her, man!" as if the Scrabble letters had come to life and followed him down here to the rec center.

If she wanted me to, I totally would. His inner bulldog had latched its jaw onto the idea of at least kissing her once. But not here. Not in front of all of Sugarplum Falls.

Mayor Lang reclaimed the microphone. "Thanks, you two. Aren't they cute as the newest couple in Sugarplum Falls? Well, make that *for the time being*. Because, ladies and gentlemen, up next is the blind date Santa hat. Get ready for some love matches!"

During the drum roll, Wyatt pulled Chelsea off the stage.

"That went better than we could have expected." Chelsea jogged after him as he tugged her through the carnival and away from the stage—before Mayor Lang could point the finger at them again.

"It was pretty combustible, if I do say so." He pulled her through the back exit from the highly decorated gymnasium, to the rear hallway. Bing Crosby's "White Christmas" and Mayor Lang's voice both muted as the door shut between them and the party.

"Maybe you can answer my question better out here." It was cooler in the hallway, but it still smelled like hot cocoa and peppermint, with a little of

Chelsea's shampoo mixed in.

"What answer?" Chelsea leaned against the brick wall, biting her lower lip. "I don't know if I remember the question." Her voice was breathy. She worked that plump lip between her teeth. Oh, she remembered all right. Despite the detour of having to sing, she was imagining their kiss right now, or Wyatt knew nothing about women.

"Chelsea." He rested a hand beside her head on the brick and moved a little closer. "You're telling me your aunt's demand that we repeat our mistletoe 'accident'didn't even make you ... *curious?*"

Her pupils dilated, and she took in a brief, sharp breath. "That was imaginary."

Undeterred, he went on. "And you're saying that by agreeing to be my temporary girlfriend, you're not willing to also enjoy all the *perks* of being my girlfriend?"

"Wyatt," she whispered.

"I like when you say my name like that, Chelsea."

Her gaze darted back and forth between his eyes. Her chin lifted, almost as if involuntarily, and her lips parted. Oh, yeah. She was definitely curious. But probably not half as curious as Wyatt.

"There's no mistletoe here, Wyatt." Chelsea's eyes left his for a split second to dart toward the ceiling.

"Do you require mistletoe?" He ran a curved finger along her jaw line. He'd spent far too many of his late-teenage hours picturing a moment very similar to this one, with Chelsea's hair cascading over one shoulder, her breath soft and shallow, wisps of sweetness and mint, while with his caress he urged her heart-rate into the *kiss me now* zone ... "Mistletoe isn't the only perfect opportunity to test out the chemistry of a first kiss, you know. There are several venues where it could happen even more naturally. Here, for instance. In this hallwa—"

A few feet down, the door to the rec room flew open. "What exactly is going on here?"

Wyatt straightened and took a giant step backward from Chelsea. "Mom?"

Chapter 7

Chelsea

Drusilla North blew in like a frozen wind. Her glower could have iced up antifreeze. "What exactly is going on here, *son?*" She said *son* like it was a dirty word. "I thought you said there would be no musical performances involved in your abandonment of my *request.*"

"What request?" Chelsea whispered. The last person Chelsea—or anyone in Sugarplum Falls—wanted to cross was Mrs. North.

"It's nothing," Wyatt said firmly.

"Nothing!" Mrs. North exploded. "You call my specific request for you to be in a certain place at a certain time nothing? I cannot believe you would lie to me."

"We were scheduled to perform." Wyatt stood with one shoulder in front of Chelsea, as if by partially hiding her he could prevent her from feeling the effects of the north wind. "We're just supporting the community."

"When you say *we*, you mean yourself and this *Sutherland* woman."

Woman? Chelsea usually still thought of herself as more of a girl. Also, only Mrs. North could make *woman* sound like a foul word as much as she could the word *son.*

"What brought you out here, Mom?" Wyatt seemed unfazed. "Chelsea and I were busy."

"Busy letting her get her hooks into you, I see." Mrs. North's frown could have touched her knees.

Chelsea's hooks? *She* was the one being hustled into a kiss. Of course, she was the one who'd needed the fake relationship, and even though it'd been

55

Wyatt's idea, Chelsea hadn't rejected it. But if she'd known how violently Mrs. North would react, Chelsea might have run away screaming instead of falling in line with the idea.

"Wyatt, honey. If you come now, I think you can still catch Rowena at the restaurant in the resort."

"You told her I was coming? And now she's being stood up? Mom, that's bad manners."

"You're the one who has the bad manners, Wyatt. You're the one standing her up." Mrs. North was speaking to Wyatt, but her eyes crawled over Chelsea like she was a bug to be squished.

What had Chelsea ever done to draw such disdain? Her guts twisted, sloshing its cups of cocoa. Chelsea backed up a few steps toward the emergency exit to the parking lot. Getting insulted by Mrs. North constituted an emergency, right? The security guards would see it that way when the door alarms sounded.

"Stop, Chelsea. You don't have to leave." Wyatt reached for her, grabbing her by the hand and squeezing hard to keep her at his side. "Mom, good night. You've done enough here. You go to dinner with Rowena, and you can tell her I'm in a relationship."

"Oh, please, Wyatt. You're only doing this to spite me. Think of all the other women out there in the world I've found who are much more suited to you and your needs and your level. Beautiful women. *Appropriate* women."

"Tell her it's a *serious* relationship."

Mrs. North's eyes widened, but they couldn't have been wider than Chelsea's. *Why was he upping the ante?* Should Chelsea feel cherished, or like she was an expendable soldier in the battle?

Plus ... battle. Since when did Wyatt North engage in battle? He was the most easy-going guy in Sugarplum Falls, and maybe in the world. *This is a side of him I've never seen. It's new. And pretty attractive.*

Chelsea tripped along after him as he tugged her away from Mrs. North, back into the rec center, across the cocoa-filled landscape, and out the front doors toward his very nice car. He held the door and helped her inside.

"Sorry about that." He flexed his fingers on the steering wheel. "She's my mom and I love her. But …" A low growl erupted and faded.

Chelsea stared through the car window at the towering town Christmas tree lit from bottom to top. There was no polite thing she could say, and it wasn't the right time to ask any of her fifty questions—like who were the other women, and what made them appropriate—and Chelsea *inappropriate*? And what exactly did Wyatt mean about their relationship being serious? Was he only baiting his mom, like she said? Most of all, why had Wyatt tried to kiss her, even though no one was watching?

That last one constituted the most perilous question, perilous to her heart.

Singing with him, just the two of them, had been alternating blasts of fire and ice. Her heart was definitely at risk.

"You're irritated," she said. "I get that. I'm irritated with Heath. How could he do that to us? Put us on the spot like that?"

Wyatt leaned against the headrest. "He did warn us."

Not directly enough! "We were so lucky Mayor Lang picked a song we knew."

"I guess we'd better prepare for the worst."

"The worst being …?"

"Heath doesn't show up for any of the rest of the performances this season."

Chelsea's heart clutched. "He wouldn't—" Except, he would. He had a baby on the way. And all those so-called *work commitments*. "But there's still the town Christmas play, if it actually happens this year, considering all the setbacks they've had at the theater, plus the Waterfall Lights." Possibly others they'd get tapped for at the last second, like always happened to Chelsea and Heath as the mayor's niece and nephew.

"The Waterfall Lights. That's in a few days."

Yep, and fifty bucks said Heath was going to stand them up for that, too. "Maybe we should head down to the falls now and see how we sound against the ice." The whole waterfall had frozen solid by now, creating its annual acoustical miracle.

"Okay." Wyatt started his car and motored down to the city park near the falls. They step-swished through the powdery snow as they crossed to the little

57

amphitheater at the base of the falls. "Oh, it's steeper than I remember." Probably because she'd never come down the steps of the amphitheater in heels before.

I haven't worn heels in a long time. Why did I tonight? Oh, right. To make Wyatt look.

His look yesterday had been such deliciousness, she couldn't resist getting another helping.

"Where should we start?" Wyatt turned her to face him. "This worked well earlier, right? Face to face?" He stood right in her personal space, lifting her arm into dance hold. "You really can't stay." He held the note, jutting his chin the tiniest bit to urge her to sing.

She did. And they danced, and the sound echoed off the frozen falls, creating a resonance that floated in the bare tree branches and sprinkled back down on them like crystals of hoar frost, the whole song through.

At the final "Baby, it's co-old out-side," Wyatt's forehead pressed against Chelsea's. His mouth was inches from hers, but his charm had swallowed her whole. Her breath heaved. This was amazing. He was amazing. She could get swept away in his everything—regardless of his mother, or Heath, or Rowena Whoever waiting for him at the resort restaurant.

"It's even better singing with just you, Chelsea." He moved his hands from dance hold and placed hers on his shoulders, and his on her hips. "We're not a bad blend, when it's cold outside."

So true. They were a good blend, in fact. Deliciously good. *I could kiss him now.*

Except—reality check. "Yeah, but it's one song, Wyatt." She had to be the voice of reason, even when he was making her head swirl like eddies of flurrying snow. "How can we develop a whole new duet repertoire after being a trio for years? Heath sings lead."

Wyatt's gaze met hers. It was deep, and his eyes were half-lidded. "I don't know, Chelsea, but it seemed to me we had an easy time of it tonight. Just you and me, singing together. It wasn't just Christmas magic that saved our moment on the stage. It was us. Long hours of singing together and we just … have something."

They did? She gulped. "I did like singing with you." *With just you.* Her voice was husky. Her gaze went to his mouth, the definition of his upper lip drawing her full attention. *If I were to lean just right, I'd feel its pressure against my lips. He knows I'm curious; he accused me of it. What if there really could be a freak mistletoe accident pushing us into igniting feelings, with or without mistletoe?*

Stars twinkled above in the dark sky, pinpricks in the black velvet.

"Heath isn't here," she breathed. It was a non-sequitur, partly. Heath wasn't here to stop her, to stop them, to tell them no. "He doesn't really get to say."

"About our repertoire?" Wyatt asked, leaning closer, the mint of his breath a caress against her cheek. "Or about ... us?"

Chelsea's heart took a whooshing ride on Santa's sleigh, snow crystals pinging every bit of her skin. He was here, and near, and he wanted to kiss her. *My teenage dream come to life.* "Um," she said, still staring at his mouth.

"You're right, Chelsea. It's up to us to make our own decisions. We're not kids."

"I never answered your question." She lifted her hands from his shoulders and laced them behind his neck. "About whether I'm curious about how it would be to kiss you."

"You've been answering that all night, just not in words, Chelsea." Wyatt leaned closer, his nose bumping against the side of hers, making her face tilt upward and her lips part, and—

A bicycle tire skidded. "Hey, that was sure sounding good." The bike rider clapped appreciatively, and the spell evaporated. Chelsea pulled her face away from Wyatt's, blinking hard and turned toward the rider, who was still talking. "That was the two of you singing, right? Very nice. You should try that professionally, or at least at some of those events. You're better than Christmas Tree-O, for sure."

Were they? Really?

The cyclist left, and Wyatt returned the full force of his attention on her. Oh, she was a nanosecond away from allowing him to change their status from singing buddies to People Who Kiss Each Other.

But no.

Curiosity had definitely seized her brain, sure, but was that a good enough reason to endanger everything Christmas Tree-O had built over the past few years? If Chelsea and Wyatt became, uh, entangled, what would happen when they *un*-entangled?

It wouldn't be pretty.

Nor would it be pretty when Heath found out they were ostensibly a couple. Being able to truthfully say nothing was going on between them was vital. Except ...

Oh, his lips had looked so delicious. And everything about him drew her, like his soul was a magnet to every particle of iron in her blood.

If Heath did show up, he'd see the change in them. He wasn't blind.

If he didn't, he could still hear the rumors, thanks to the Sutherland family network of communication.

Worse, if this was his idea of a game, and it might be, Chelsea's heart was in big trouble. Because Wyatt, with his charm, had the most game over her she'd ever seen. He put Fargo Frye a distant second place; no, not even on the scoreboard.

Oh, I could so easily believe this lie and be the biggest loser.

"You'd better take me back to my car." Chelsea pulled out of his grasp and headed for the car. That was close. Too close. And he definitely had the power to endanger her feelings. *I'm not ready for a heartbreak. I haven't even healed from the last one.* "I'll see you at our next practice."

"Chelsea—"

"Wyatt. It can't happen. We have to tell Heath. Stat."

Heath would help her see the forest for the trees, if nothing else worked to protect her heart.

Chapter 8

Wyatt

Wyatt paced his office at North Star Capital. The last thing he wanted to do was drag Heath Sutherland into his current dilemma. But a dilemma it was. He plucked an ornament from the little Christmas tree on his desk and juggled it, then caught it in his hand and gripped hard.

"Does she want me or not?" he asked aloud.

Yes, a big yes, and then no, a hard no, thanks to his mom. And then yes again. And then another solid no after that night biker interrupted their moment and inadvertently threw Heath into the way of their kiss.

After that, Chelsea had insisted he take her back to the rec center so she could help clean up the Hot Cocoa Festival with the rest of the Sutherlands—and she'd refused to let him come in and assist.

At least I'm making her a little uncomfortable.

Except ... why was he? Why was that his sudden goal, putting Chelsea Sutherland off her game, getting her to pull down her walls and kiss him? It wasn't just because he'd had this pent up curiosity of his own about her kiss for too long to count the days. It wasn't just to spite his mother, no matter what Drusilla and Deacon North must be concluding behind Wyatt's back.

Why now? Why did Wyatt suddenly want her so much—because when the Heath-cat's away, the mice will play? Obviously it intrigued him. The danger of the game, of dating his best friend's suddenly-hot-and-needy little sister while older brother wasn't looking. That definitely had merit as a theory, but it certainly wouldn't reflect well on Wyatt's character if that were the case.

Then again, not much of anything in Wyatt's dating past reflected well on his character.

When I think about being with Chelsea, I don't want to be that guy anymore. I'm done being the guy who kisses any girl who hits on me just to make her happy for an hour. Those girls mean nothing to me. But Chelsea isn't those girls.

Last night, for instance, he'd full-on ignored that *call me* girl. Usually, he at least ended up with a couple of phone numbers after a singing gig. Every girl in town seemed to want to date the bachelor heir to the bank with the velvet voice. Or, okay, at least the nice backup voice.

"You're going to wear a rut in the rug. Mrs. North won't like it." Mack came in and plopped in one of the chairs. "My kids said you and Chelsea almost stepped on their Candy Kingdom war the other night. I somehow missed seeing you there. Aunt Rita was telling me a few tidbits about people in town. I couldn't break away." He put his feet up on the windowsill. As always. This time, he toppled one of the potted poinsettias, scattering potting soil on the sill.

"Watch it." Wyatt righted it. Honestly, poinsettias were Mrs. Sutherland's favorite flower, so Mom shouldn't decorate with them if she didn't want Wyatt thinking about the Sutherlands. "Don't you have accounts to review?"

"Don't you?" Mack laced his fingers behind his head. "From what I hear, you still haven't pinpointed the bank's next investment. Not only will you make somebody's Christmas when you announce it, you'll also start making a profit. A penny loaned is a penny that's earning interest."

Or so the old North Star Bank mantra had gone, back when they loaned to local businesses. But Grandpa's mantra had had an addendum to it: *A penny loaned is a penny that's earning interest for us and building someone else's future.*

"So what are you holding back for?"

Yeah. Why? "Same as always. The numbers aren't adding up."

"Because you're not using the calculator. They balance, dude. You just have to put them into the equations."

Annnnnd that was where Wyatt's skill set ended. "I can rule out several, based on principle."

"Whoa, there." Mack held up his palms. "Who said anything about principle? This is North Star Capital. We focus on a different *p* word: *profit.*"

62

"Oh, stop." He'd said it before, and he'd repeat himself into his grave. "I want to invest this capital locally."

Mack waved him away. "Be specific. Locally, as in Sugarplum Falls? Or in the whole state? Because I know a couple of investment firm owners down the hall who would prefer the latter."

"Local-local. The closer the better." He was a broken record, and it was like no one else in the whole financial firm could hear his point anymore.

"Dude. Your whole future is on the line with this. You're not really in a position to take moral stands of supporting the community right now. There's more at stake. Once you've got your cushy job as one-third owner of North Star Capital and the VP title, *then* you can start dishing out meal tickets to the local peasants."

No. Unless he stood up to them from the beginning, he wouldn't be strong enough. He had to begin as he meant to go on. They couldn't see him as their laid-back, chill son anymore. The go-along-to-get-along guy. This was too much money to just throw away to other communities when it could be used to improve Sugarplum Falls.

Wyatt crushed the Christmas ornament in his fist, indenting the plastic on one side. "You've been hanging out with my mother too much."

"She's a very attractive woman." Mack waggled his eyebrows, but then went serious. "Hey, cool down. I'm just spouting what gets beaten into us in every staff meeting and every company email. Build the firm's equity. Build the assets and the reputation. Build our future."

Sure, sure.

"Forget about the scruples and just crunch the numbers, Wyatt."

Wyatt grimaced and finished crushing the plastic ball into oblivion. *We're Norths. We're numbers people.* Mom's mantra. *That's why we win.* She'd always looped Wyatt into her declaration, but was she blind? Or did she just think that wishing and shouting it often enough would make it so?

He'd never live up to that fantasy Mom and Dad had for him.

"Fine. I know what you're thinking again, that numbers aren't your forte." Mack got up and started pacing Wyatt's carpet rut. "Think, think. If only you knew someone with a mathematical mind. If only you had a close

63

enough relationship with that person that you could call upon her skills as a favor. If only you were *publicly dating* that person, and could use her help to then justify to your bank-owning mother the merit of your dating decision."

"What do you mean publicly dating?"

"Dude. Word doesn't travel slowly in the Sutherland family. Plus, I was at the Hot Cocoa Festival Saturday night. I saw the sparks zapping between the two of you when Mayor Lang cajoled you into singing that uncomfortable song. You made *all* of us uncomfortable. Some of us needed *just a cigarette more*." He followed it with a *ho-ho-ho* and a pat of his belly.

Mack didn't smoke, whether or not he quoted outdated lyrics. "Knock it off, Mack."

"Don't dismiss my idea. Chelsea could take one look at the compiled research on your list and point to the exact company you should invest in. It'd take her less time than Santa's trip down the chimney."

True. "I don't know. It'd be like I was using her."

"Pah! As if she's not using you."

"What makes you say that?"

"Oh, please. Not that I've breathed a word to anyone, including my wife, but when you were asking about Fargo as Chelsea's ex, and then we got our invitation to Fargo and Esther's wedding, and then I suddenly saw you and Chelsea together, with Chelsea sporting a sexy vintage makeover, I put the clues together. Myself. I'm not as dumb as I look. There's a reason your parents keep me around at the North Star Capital." He tapped his temple.

Wyatt's stomach clenched. If Mack had put it together, had anyone else? Probably not, since they hadn't been privy to Wyatt's questions about Fargo. Nevertheless, no way could Wyatt let Chelsea endure any form of further humiliation, like being accused of faking having a boyfriend. He'd better step up his game and make their relationship as convincing as possible.

If she'd let him.

"I'm not going to use her."

"That's up to you. Quid pro quo, my friend."

"It's different."

"Is it?" Was it?

Chapter 9

Chelsea

Ah, Waterfall Lights was the best night of the year in Sugarplum Falls. Hands down.

The lights danced in reds and greens on the translucent, reflective sheet of ice the waterfall had become in the subzero temps. Jazzy Christmas music played, and timed light patterns created pictures of Santa sliding down the chimney, a Christmas tree with presents, and dozens of other little displays.

The town of Sugarplum Falls knew how to put on a show. Cars were lined up in the parking lot to watch the show and tune in to the music on a short-distance signal over the radio. Others had ventured out and were filling the entire amphitheater to hear the live performances of the Sugarplum Falls High School orchestra playing selections from *The Nutcracker,* the local wannabe actress doing a dramatic reading, and a chorus of little kids singing "Here Comes Santa Claus."

But they were all just the warm up. Chelsea and Wyatt—Christmas Tree-O, *sans Heath* due to alleged *work commitments* again—were supposedly the main attraction.

Again, though, their past three days of song practices over cyber-connections with Heath had been extremely brief, on account of Chelsea's body chemistry being far too susceptible to Wyatt's, and out of fear that Heath would be able to read them if they stayed on camera too long with him.

Chelsea patted her arms to stave off the cold. This coat was not enough of a shield against this year's cold snap in Sugarplum Falls. "If only they could move the Waterfall Lights concert inside for once. Which, obviously, would defeat the purpose." None of the gathered audience seemed as thoroughly chilled as Chelsea, but of course they were huddled together.

"You want my scarf?" Wyatt unwound the red polar fleece from his neck. "I'm not even cold."

Liar. "Thanks." She couldn't resist it, just like she couldn't resist Wyatt. He was just so ... everything. *I can't let him near me. If I smell his aftershave, I will kiss him.*

Wyatt stepped close and placed the soft fabric around her shoulders, tugging her slightly closer to him in the process. Gently, he wound it around her neck in a loose wrap. The scent of his aftershave wafted from the scarf to her senses, enveloping her in a Wyatt-scented cloud, his wintergreen kisses dancing in her imagination.

Yikes! No!

"Oh, you'll get too cold." She reached to remove the intoxicating fabric.

"What?" Wyatt stepped back.

Chelsea whipped the scarf off, not without taking one last sniff, and pushed it back into his hands. "Besides, we're both wearing black coats and red scarves. It'd look weird not to match. Everyone else in the show is matching. It's our uniform. And we have to look like we're together. Uh—as an act, I mean. Not as a couple, since we haven't even looped Heath in yet, and we have to, soon. I mean, I mean ..."

Fortunately for Chelsea's freak-out, their turn came up to sing just then. They started with "Winter Wonderland"—a back-and-forth duet like their Hot Cocoa Festival rendition that had been so well-received. It went well even without practice. Wyatt's voice poured over her like melted hot fudge sauce, getting into all her crevices and making her all gooey.

When he sang the part about Parson Brown asking if they were married, Chelsea fully succumbed to the imaginary moment.

Refocus. Pretend you're singing karaoke, not live and in person with the Charm Machine. Yeah, and she'd better also pretend she didn't wish the wonderland moment could come true.

"Have Yourself a Merry Little Christmas" was next, a little more sedate. They ended the set with "Christmas Kisses," and Wyatt kissed the tip of her nose at the end of the song.

The crowd went wild.

Chelsea's tummy's elf workshop went wilder. Every single one of them set off their wind-up toys at once, setting her nerve endings inside and out afire.

They bowed, and Chelsea gave Wyatt a tight smile. "I'll see you at the Christmas play."

"But—"

She couldn't stay for buts. She had to bolt.

Kisses were infectious, more than the flu. Even nose-tip kisses. At least they were to her emotions.

She fled.

A few days later, at the opening night performance of the town Christmas play, that had been significantly revised, according to rumors, Chelsea and Wyatt met in the wings backstage in the Kingston Theater, which was looking remarkably shabby after last year's flood. The curtains were even askew— much like Chelsea's hormones as Wyatt stood inches from her, filling her with all kinds of delirium.

"You ready?" she asked.

"Are we ever? We should get together and practice so this doesn't happen again."

No. Nope.

Mayor Lang introduced them again.

"And now, ladies and gentlemen, as our opening act, a Sugarplum Falls treasure that you've all enjoyed for the past ten Christmases running— Christmas Tree-O!"

"Minus Heath Sutherland," Chelsea said as she took the microphone. "You'll be happy to know that Heath *will* definitely be in town at our next performance and you'll get the full trio treatment. For now, it's just Wyatt and me as the duo. Please, try to enjoy it anyway."

A voice rose up from somewhere in the darkened seats of the Kingston Theater. "Why don't you kiss her for real this time and not just on the tip of her nose, Wyatt?"

"Yeah," another heckler hollered. "Do I have to bring some mistletoe onstage myself to get any real Christmas magic going?"

"We want a real kiss! None of this nose stuff! It's weak!"

This town was full of pushy meddlers. They probably had nothing better to do than to watch those cheesy holiday romance movies all day and night from Halloween on. They probably watched reality dating shows all the other months, too.

Wyatt, however, wore the kind of jaunty grin that said he didn't mind the love-pushers one bit. In fact, he might even enjoy it.

Blast him. That jaunty grin of his sent her into heart throbs every time he used it on her. Even when he used it on other people. She was such a sucker!

The music struck up—a familiar song they'd done a thousand times with Heath, but now they had to turn it into a duet. Wyatt sang the words about dreaming of a white Christmas, nostalgic, and homey. His voice was rich and pure, at least as delicious as Bing Crosby's. Maybe more, since it was being directed solely at her, and accompanied by soulful glances from Wyatt North. The air around Chelsea swirled like a warm mist of love, stealing her thoughts.

Chelsea's turn came on the second stanza. She echoed with the verse about writing Christmas cards, while everything else in the room faded away, and it was just Wyatt and Chelsea in the room. No spectators, just the two of them and Chelsea's imagination.

Among the glistening of the treetops, she sang about the children that listened for sleigh bells in the snow, and a panorama stretched before her mind's eye, the pretty picture the song's lyrics painted, with Chelsea and Wyatt and their future family featured in every scene. Little children, all with Chelsea's dark hair and Wyatt's bright grin, gathered at cozy cottage windows, watching for Santa.

Ah, wouldn't days like that be merry and bright?

Together they harmonized, until Wyatt took the phrase with the song's deepest wish that all her Christmases be white. Holding out the last note, he leaned in on the last phrase and kissed Chelsea on her temple.

Her eyes floated shut. "Merry Christmas, Wyatt," she whispered. Then, she tilted her chin up and kissed his cheek.

Another song began immediately. Right! She popped back to life as the audience tittered at her swoon.

Her very, very public swoon.

If this little display of their relationship didn't get back to Heath, nothing would.

When the songs finally ended, Chelsea fled, this time yanking Wyatt back into the wings of the theater, ignoring all the pre-production prop-setup being done by the stage crew, and not caring who heard her.

"We can't go another day without telling Heath." He was one of them. Part of the trio. They were doing this behind his back, and he deserved to not be the last to know, even if he wasn't in Sugarplum Falls anymore full time. He was Wyatt's best friend, and Chelsea's only brother. For all his faults, Heath was her best friend, too. Maybe second-best, after Wyatt, make that.

"Tell Heath about what? About how much I'm falling for you?"

Chelsea lurched to an emotional halt. She stared at him, giving that jolly smile of his a hard peer.

Truth or dare—that's what his statement had seemed like.

A test. One she could fail with the least breath. Her heart was begging her, *Believe him.*

Except, Wyatt North was the best actor when it came to getting girls to fall for him, and had been for years. There'd been Allison, Beth, Carlene, Darienne, Evvie, Faline, Gretchen, Hailey, Imelda, Julie ... The alphabet of women's names going through his revolving door went on. Frankly, Chelsea had had a front row seat to his love-her-and-leave-her ways, and she was far too smart to fall for the ruse.

Oh, but she was so vulnerable to it, too.

I can barely resist him when he's not at close range. Being this near, having him sing words of love to me, and act like he means it, telling people I'm his girlfriend, telling his mom we're in a serious relationship, telling my Mom *we're seeing each other ... I'm so toasted, roasted, and something else that rhymes with -oasted.*

"We'd better have this discussion elsewhere." She marched toward the backstage exit and out into the cold behind the theater near the parking lot.

"How about at the Falls Overlook?"

Make-out point? Seriously? "Wyatt!"

Wyatt took off his scarf and wrapped it tenderly around her neck. Again. Like he remembered the effect it'd had on her last time, and he was just fine using her weakness against her.

"Okay, if you'd rather stand out here in the cold, when you could sit in my warm car, listening to good music, taking in the view of the falls so that you can have the most comfortable circumstances possible to have this important discussion, that's fine by me."

Had he deliberately spritzed the scarf with his manly pheromones just to turn her brain to goo so that he could bend her to his will?

"That does sound better than out here in the cold." She relented and got into the passenger side of his car. Oh, the leather seats were heated, and the car warmed instantly. She thawed, and her spine relaxed against the seat of the car.

Maybe it was all right, this ruse. Maybe Heath wouldn't mind too much.

Wyatt took a turn onto Orchard Avenue, his car's handling taking each bend in the winding road between town and the orchard with ease. It soothed Chelsea even more. Yeah, things weren't as cold and bleak as they'd felt a second ago. Wyatt was great. He was helping. They were building up a visual history of proof of their relationship for Chelsea's benefit. He was smart, and kind, and helpful—as well as being irresistibly doused in aftershave made of pine and cucumber and sandalwood.

"I know why you're nervous." Wyatt slowed down on a turn that headed up toward the canyon.

"If you think I'm scared to kiss you it's …" What? True? But maybe not for the reasons he was thinking? "I'm not."

"Really? That's great to hear, but not the direction I was going."

Chelsea sat forward. "Say, what direction *are* we going, here?"

"Over the canyon."

"To where?"

"You'll see."

Um, what was going on? But soon, they pulled into the neighboring town of Reindeer Crossing. It was about the same size as Sugarplum Falls, but it had a different vibe. More eclectic. And a lot more skiers from out of town.

Wyatt parked the car in front of a line of shops. At this hour, all the storefronts were dark—except one.

"What's going on, Wyatt?"

"The wedding is in less than two weeks' time."

Already! How could it have come up on Chelsea so quickly? She'd been furiously working every day on the medical studies that needed to be completed before year-end and avoiding personal visits from Wyatt every night. That's how.

"I can't go. I can't see them."

Make that she couldn't see *him*. Not like this. Not having already exhausted every cute vintage item from Grandma's closet during her public appearances.

"I told you, success is the best revenge."

"What does a store in Reindeer Crossing have to do with anything like that?" Chelsea wanted to hug her legs to her chest and put her head down onto her knees and never look up again. "Please say this little shop has a portal to another dimension, and when we emerge from it, it'll be next year, and every Sutherland will just be super glad to find us alive with the mystery solved of your abandoned car."

Wyatt reached for her hand and gently pried her fingers out of their clench. "Come on in. I'll show you." He lifted her fingertips to his lips and kissed them so lightly it might have been an angel's caress.

Again, Chelsea couldn't breathe. She could die of asphyxiation at this rate. Strangled by desire. *I sound like a terrible pulp novel from the 1940s.*

Oxygen-deprived, she followed him inside Crossing Clothiers.

"Meet Amélie and Gregor."

The two shop-owners more or less kowtowed to Wyatt, for whatever reason, but they brought batch after batch of clothes for Chelsea to try on.

No matter what Amélie or Gregor chose and draped over her, Chelsea felt like a model. How? Piece after piece were so pretty and a fitted black silk one definitely looked amazing on her, but Wyatt kept waving them away until a burgundy silk dress—a wrap style with a v-neck and a wide black velvet belt—stopped the show.

"Now *that's* what I call a dress. I hereby dub it the Fargo Slayer."

Chelsea stared into the mirror. For a second, she might not argue with Kaden and Jaidyn. In this gown, she did look like Barbie's dark-haired friend, except ready for a Christmas party.

And ready to upstage the blonde.

Was that a good idea? Did she really care about what Fargo thought?

Very much. Too much. Stupid-much.

"Wyatt, it's beautiful. They all are, but—"

"Agreed. We'll take all of them." He waved his hand in a *wrap them up, Jeeves,* circle at Gregor.

"All!" But—Chelsea couldn't afford all of them. Well, she could, but she shouldn't. Her clothing budget for the past many months had been nil, and, oh. They were gorgeous, but she shouldn't get them. Even though everything she'd tried on was like it had been designed specifically for her body's measurements and her skin and hair coloring.

"Hold on a second, Wyatt. Let me just add up some numbers after I look at the price tags."

Wyatt went to the counter with his platinum credit card and shushed Chelsea's retorts. Gregor placed everything in pretty tissue paper, and Amélie placed them all in gold-embossed boxes.

When they took the bags out to the car, he said, "Gregor and Amélie are clients of North Star Capital." As if that explained everything.

"So, they give you a clothing discount?" They headed out of town, back toward the mountain pass.

"They kind of owed me a favor, and I wanted to call it in, so they'd stop wondering when I'd show up."

"Oh." There was probably more to it, but she'd have to wait to find out. Chelsea reached inside the bag and tugged out a corner of the burgundy dress. It was so pretty, and it made her feel pretty. *And Wyatt makes me feel pretty.* "Why did you do this?"

He looked straight out at the road. His fingers flexed on the steering wheel. "Has anyone ever told you that you look good in burgundy?"

Maybe once or twice. She shrugged. "How can I ever thank you?"

"Don't ask me that right now."

Huh. Why not? "But you'll tell me eventually?"

Wyatt headed them back down the road toward Sugarplum Falls. The road wound along the Sugar River, and glimpses of the shining frozen river popped from between the trees in the moonlight now and then. "Tell me something, Chelsea. When was the last time you went shopping?"

"This afternoon. I picked up milk and another carton of eggnog."

"Clothes shopping."

"Oh." Chelsea looked out the other window. "It's been a while, I guess."

"More than a year?" When she was quiet, he pressed, "More than two years?"

The memory flooded back to her. "The dress was aquamarine organza, with a flowing skirt that made me feel tall and willowy and feminine. I almost felt beautiful. I bought something nice to wear the night I thought Fargo Frye was going to propose to me."

To her left, a grinding of teeth sounded. She turned. Wyatt's temples were pulsating. Finally, one word croaked through. "Propose?"

"Or so I thought."

He was quiet for a moment, as if swallowing a half dozen responses before choosing one. "You were going to turn him down, I hope."

Chelsea angled away again, and in a low voice spoke a thumbnail version of the truth—truth spiked with barbs. "He ... wasn't honest with me. I took the dress back."

"And started wearing the Gray Sweats of Shame."

Speaking of barbs! "Back off, Wyatt." How could he know how it felt to be strung along and then not just rejected but also mocked? He was Wyatt North, the guy every girl threw herself at, but who never got emotionally involved. The devil-may-care Mr. Aloofness who cast aside girls like empty soda cans. Sweet but finished.

"That's not what I meant, Chelsea."

How else was she supposed to take it?

He pulled over to the side of the road, just as they came up to Holly Berry House's turnoff, but he didn't make his way up the drive. "How did you feel tonight? With me?"

She turned to him. "I—I don't know." She squeezed her eyes shut. Gorgeous, protected, cherished? The adjectives streamed through. "Good until you brought up my working-from-home wardrobe."

He reached for her. He touched her chin and guided her face toward him, and then waited. At last she peeked open an eye. "Even when you're in sweats, no woman in that room tomorrow can possibly hold a candle to you. You're Chelsea Sutherland."

Chelsea blinked, searching his face for any sign of insincerity. He couldn't mean that. He was just trying to boost her confidence. *It's working.* He wore the same thirsty look he'd worn in the hallway at the rec center the other night, the one that made Chelsea wishful-thinkingly believe he was thinking about kissing her.

I'm thinking about kissing him. Okay, that's not new. That's basically my day and night. When I'm working through mathematical conundrums at work, it's distracting me. Maybe I should just kiss him to get it out of my system. Then I could just go on with life, and—

Her phone buzzed. "It's my mom."

Wyatt sat back against the seat, and Chelsea picked up, the tension between them drained away.

"Chelsea? Can you walk over from the cottage and help me? My computer is blinking the words *virus, virus, virus,* and I've got company here and I can't get anything ordered and it's Christmas and there's a wedding at my house in less than two weeks, but with the rehearsal dinner first, and I'm going crazy."

Mom could definitely go into frantic mode. "I'll be right there." Chelsea tapped the dash and turned to Wyatt. "Home, James. The math geek has received her Bat Signal." Being asked to fix a computer virus shouldn't trigger Chelsea to feel ugly all over again. It wasn't even the same as being asked to do someone's math homework. And yet ... *Thanks a lot, Fargo.*

"Your house home? Good, because I've got a Scrabble word to play."

"Holly Berry House proper."

"Oh." His voice went flat. "All right. It was a combination of two words anyway. You might not have allowed it." They pulled up at the driveway of the big house, lights ablaze inside, despite the late hour, and an unfamiliar car in the drive, new and shiny. "Heath wouldn't have stood for it for a second, believe me."

"Well, I'm not Heath. As you know. You might have to try me on the Scrabble words later. I can be flexible."

Wyatt's brow shot up, as if she'd just inadvertently said something with a double entendre. "Quit tormenting me, Chelsea."

Tormenting him! She got out and marched across the snow-covered gravel to the house, leaving Wyatt in his car, and burst into the house. "Mom? Are you—"

But her words died on the warm air because there, on the front room sofa, grinned ... *Fargo and Esther?*

Chelsea's tongue swelled up at the back of her throat, closing off her breathing, and not in a *Wyatt steals my oxygen* kind of way.

"If it isn't little Chelsea." Esther smirked and tilted her highly processed blonde head to the side, placing a possessive hand on Fargo's thigh, as if to flaunt the enormous diamond on her left ring finger. The gem was so huge it could have taken the place of the obligatory orange at the toe of anyone's Christmas stocking. Chelsea blanched. "So nice of you to come the second we beckoned."

Fargo chortled. "I trained Chelsea well."

The furniture spun, maybe from entering a hot room after being in the starkly cold night. Or maybe not. She grabbed for a nearby support, but none came to hand.

Fargo, so sardonic. Esther, so smug.

Chelsea, so off-balance she might topple.

Fargo's gaze crawled up and down Chelsea's frame, padded by ten pounds of puffy parka, and he slightly shook his head, as if to say, *I can't believe I ever forced myself to pretend to be into that lump of gunk.*

How could Mom have summoned Chelsea here with no warning about the people who constituted "company?" Chelsea hadn't braced herself for impact. *I have to get out of here.* Chelsea took a giant step backward, but she bumped into Wyatt's firm chest.

Chapter 10

Wyatt

"**H**ello." Wyatt placed both hands on Chelsea's arms. She'd wobbled, and no wonder. "If it isn't the happy couple." More like the haughty couple. "What brought you to town so soon before your wedding?"

Fargo sneered. "If it isn't the singing banker and his friend's little sister."

"Our rehearsal dinner tomorrow. For our wedding, of course." Esther frowned and side-eyed Fargo Frye. "How do you know Wyatt North?"

"Professionally," Fargo said. Really, the jerk should have said *unprofessionally,* considering Fargo's behavior at the banking conference, the way he'd been hitting on those cocktail waitresses. "Back when I was hunting for investors for my startup, North Star Capital happened to be at the same conference." Where Wyatt had kept Fargo Frye well away from his parents, who were the sole decision-makers for the capital group at the time. "Small firm, small town, small potatoes. I hooked a bigger investor for Tingle Toes, of course."

For that novelty sock business? Really? "I hadn't heard." Wyatt leveled a gaze on Fargo. "It's not a huge community, so word usually gets around. Who was your backer?"

"Oh, that. Well ..."

Ah. So the deal had fallen apart. Never mind. "Don't worry. Happens all the time."

Esther raked a gaze over Chelsea. "Been getting plenty to eat these days, I see, Chelsea."

What was she hinting at? Oh, the puffy coat? It did hide Chelsea's almost-too-lean figure.

"Chelsea always did like a hearty meal." Fargo gave a faint pig-snort.

"Didn't ya, Chelse?"

Chelse. The pet name grated, knuckles on an old metal washboard. Wyatt's fingers pressed harder into her upper arms, possibly hurting her despite the layers of down in her parka. Chelsea was still frozen in Wyatt's grip. She hadn't muttered a peep.

"Oh, Fargo, we should leave the poor thing alone. Can't you see? Just laying eyes on you is putting her into a trance." Esther turned back to Chelsea. "Let's go easy on her. She probably hasn't had a date since you dumped her. Look at her, for heaven's sake. My mom says the girl hasn't cut her hair and she's been wearing the same clothes for a year and a half."

Not true! "Knock it off, Esther." Wyatt relaxed his grip and turned Chelsea toward him. "Watch it. You're talking about my fiancée there."

Good grief. Why had that word flown out of Wyatt's mouth? But it had. And now he couldn't suck it back. It was doing five hundred laps around the room like it belonged in Indianapolis in a Formula One car. But he couldn't stand hearing them slight her. She possessed ten times their intellectual prowess and was a thousand times kinder and prettier than Esther. Plus, she had more integrity in her little finger than Fargo had in his entire body—or even in his imagination of himself.

Wyatt dug in his heels. He was doing this thing. However, he didn't risk peeking down at Chelsea's reaction. It might throw him off.

"You're engaged?" Fargo's neck snapped backward. "To *him?*"

"You bet she is. Isn't that right, Chelsea?" He waited for her to affirm, and she nodded dumbly, like she'd been struck by an EMP and only her muscular systems remained in working order, but not her vocal cords.

"I don't believe it." Esther crossed her arms over her sizeable chest that spilled out of her too-tight sweater, and not in the fetching way Chelsea's had in the vintage dress at the hot cocoa tasting night. "I'm a Sutherland. I would have heard by now if that was one bit true."

Good point. Wyatt thought fast, but not as fast as Esther's tongue.

"How much is Chelsea paying you to say this? It's obviously a lie. I'll bet the two of you, who are clearly more like brother and sister and have been for *years*, haven't even kissed. The thought!" She made a gagging sound. "Who else is hearing this baloney with me?" She looked around as though she were in a crowded room, but it was only the four of them. "Am I the only one calling BS?"

A sudden thrashing pulled Chelsea out of Wyatt's grasp, and she turned toward him. Taking off her coat, she dropped it at her feet, revealing her figure-hugging red sweater, which she'd worn for their performance at the Christmas play, and which had scored the wolf whistles.

A low *whoa* emanated from Fargo's end of the couch. "That's hot. Chelsea, Chelsea, Chelsea." Right in front of Esther, too.

However, Wyatt's eyes were riveted on Chelsea's, and she was devouring him with their deep blue depths.

"Yes," she whispered, her tones low and husky and shooting tingles all over Wyatt's skin. "And I can't wait for our wedding night."

Now the *whoa* came from Wyatt's throat, but it was curtailed because Chelsea took his face in both hands, rose up on tiptoe and touched her soft, supple lips to his. Wyatt's eyes drifted shut, and all he became was the kiss. Bonfires crackled, shooting orange and red sparks into an endless night sky, drawing his soul to the heavens, twirling him until his head spun along with the torrent of desire churning in his veins. Her mouth moved expertly, as if trained to specifically touch each of his most incendiary nerves. A little moan rose in his throat, and her breaths brushed his cheek between kisses.

Wyatt's arms found their way to her narrow rib cage, and then to her spine, where he pulled her closer, breathing her mix of mint and florals, every sense—taste, touch, smell, sound, sight—suddenly alive as if for the first time.

Chelsea deepened the kiss, and Wyatt welcomed the increase in passion with a return of his own. He couldn't pull her close enough to him, her curves pressing against his torso, her tiny waist almost easy to encircle with his grasp, fingertip to fingertip, but with his hands still resting on her full hips. Oh, she was divine, a gift from the heavens above, and this angelic kiss was so much more than Wyatt could ever deserve, like getting a car on Christmas morning before he even earned a driver's license.

But it wasn't just the amazingness of her kissing skills, even though they were expert beyond anything he'd ever experienced, and he'd experienced a lot of kisses. It couldn't just be the kisses. *It's more. It's ... her. It's how I feel when she looks at me that way, like I want to be the man she thinks I am.*

Kissing Chelsea Sutherland took kissing to a whole different level. It wasn't the body, but the spirit plus the body—which, did they call that the soul? Everything about him wanted to own this kiss, to own her, to own himself and them as a combination. To never stop kissing her because—

"Ahem." Someone beside them was obviously uncomfortable. Wyatt didn't even crack an eye, and since Chelsea didn't dial down any of her kiss's passion, neither would he.

"A heh-heh-heh-hem."

Forget it. No chance was Wyatt stopping the throes of this kiss to satisfy the comfort of those two cretins on the couch. Not this kiss, not for them. He lifted his hand and ran it through the silken strands of Chelsea's hair. How had he never let this happen before? How had he never taken this chance even once out of the hundreds of times he'd been alone with her?

He'd been living beneath his potential joy. But no more. Never again.

This girl was his fiancée, and she'd said yes, and she'd begged for a wedding night, and by gum, she was going to get one—and soon—if she kept revving Wyatt's engines this way, and—

"Cease and desist this instant." The voice got louder, and definitely more demanding. "If the two of you can get ahold of yourselves and your childish display, don't we have some practicing to do for Christmas Tree-O?"

Heath.

Chapter 11

Chelsea

"Heath!" Chelsea pulled her hot, raw lips away from Wyatt's. She dragged the back of her hand across her face to catch any stray moisture. Oh, that kiss! She was going to need to hold onto something. But it couldn't be Wyatt—not with Heath watching.

"I can see the two of you have been busy doing some Christmas shopping—in each other's personal space bubbles."

Chelsea blinked to clear her blurred vision. "What are you doing here?" she finally managed. Fargo and Esther were no longer in the room. Uh, they'd probably exited a few minutes ago, the second the kiss got heated and Chelsea's world turned into an episode of *Falls Landing,* that teen soap opera.

"Why are you looking at me like I just flew in from the moon? Mom did tell you she had company. As in, it's *me.* The rehearsal dinner and the wedding are being held here, you know of course. Hence the *other* house guests who are here." He frowned. "Look, I told her not to say it was me. I wanted to surprise you." He aimed his index finger at Chelsea. "You, not *you.*" He wagged the finger between the two of them. "But I guess I'm the one who got the surprise." If his frown had grown any deeper, it would have looked like a Confucius mustache.

"So you're okay with it." Wyatt—the fool—pasted on a dashing smile. "Your sister and me, I mean."

Uh, no. Could Wyatt read nothing? "Wyatt ..."

"Okay with it!" Heath roared. "We have been through this for *years*, Wyatt. Come talk to me alone. I don't think my little sister should hear what I have to say to you."

"Heath. I'm twenty-seven."

"No." Heath jerked Wyatt by the arm and marched him back outside, slamming the door with a whoosh of snow flowing onto the tile entryway.

Chelsea stood stock still. Now and then, indecipherable pops of yelling came through the plate-glass window and punctuated the air. *All in Heath's voice.* She shivered, and not from the cold night.

"Chelsea?" Mom stood at her side, her warmth radiating. "What's this I'm hearing from your cousin Esther? Engaged?"

Chelsea looked up. Mom's face wasn't what she expected. Her features were bunched together in hurt.

"Mom—it's not ..." Not what? What Mom thought? Not what Chelsea thought fifteen minutes ago? Everything was morphing and changing, like the colored plastic snowflakes inside one of those twisting kaleidoscopes Chelsea used to receive in her stocking every Christmas. "I'm not sure what to say."

"Do you love him?"

Ooh, now she really didn't know what to say. "He's kinder to me than any man has been in years." That was true. "We've known each other a long time. Heath was always there, though." Telling us *look at each other and die.* "For all I know Heath could be ripping Wyatt limb from limb out there."

"According to Esther, your dad could be ripping Wyatt limb from limb right now—for the way he was ravishing you in public. If a man does that in public, what's he doing in private, dear?"

Their first kiss! Yeah, not what she would have planned—in full view of her ex and Esther. Not exactly ideal, but then again, it far exceeded any expectations, or even any dreams. Kissing Wyatt North was like taking off in a rocket ship, with all the G-forces shooting her into the stratosphere.

"Are you even listening? You look dazed. Like you, my math-minded daughter, are not being logical at all." Mom raised a skeptical eyebrow. "I very much hope you're being more cautious than you seem right now."

Caution hadn't been in her skill set in the past half hour. Half an hour ago, Chelsea had never even kissed the guy. *Then all of a sudden I'm telling him I'm raring for a wedding night.*

Of course, that had to have been the Fargo-Esther pressure.

The reaction from Fargo had been choice. But poor Esther. *Who'd have thought I'd think that ever.* Then again, Esther and the unexpected often went together. Who'd have thought Chelsea and Esther—the family's *two peas in a pod* as kids, ice skating partners who begged for matching dolls for Christmas so they could play together year-round—would have ended up as teens and adults with Esther forever ripping on Chelsea, and then getting stuck with Chelsea's disgusting ex?

"Don't worry, Mom. Heath is probably talking Wyatt out of the whole thing right now." Letting his clenched fists do the talking. Yeah, Heath wasn't exactly a serial guy-puncher, but when riled, stay out of his way. "I'm really sorry we haven't gone about it the right way. Will you forgive me?"

Mom rubbed her forehead and gathered Chelsea into a hug. "Sweetheart. There's nothing to forgive. You know we love Wyatt. I guess it's just that we never imagined the two of you together because of certain family considerations. It's new. It's not unwelcome. There's a difference."

Was there? Mom might not be mad, but she definitely didn't show enthusiasm. And what did *certain family considerations* mean? Still, Chelsea relaxed into Mom's embrace—until the door flung open and in marched Heath.

"Excuse me, Mom. I need to speak with my *sister.*"

Heath hustled Chelsea over to the Christmas tree in the corner and lowered his voice. At least he wasn't making her stand in the cold for this tongue lashing. "What exactly do you think you're doing?"

"What *exactly* are you referring to?" To the fact that she always promised not to date Wyatt and now she was ostensibly engaged to him? "We're not dating. We're engaged."

"You're *ruining* Christmas Tree-O is what I'm referring to." He stomped his foot. "Do you know how long I've dedicated myself to making it a success? How many hours I've put into creating a brand for us?"

Uh, what? Heath was the one ruining the trio by never showing up for either practices or performances. Hello.

"Heath, have you been getting enough sleep at night? Is Odessa keeping you awake with false labor pains? Because you're non-sequituring all over the place."

"No, I'm not. If you date Wyatt, the dynamic of Christmas Tree-O shifts irrevocably. Stop *now* before things go too far. If you guys are kissing like that in public, what's going on in private?" He shook his head.

"It's not what you think." If only he knew how little had gone on in private, but Chelsea wasn't *not* kissing and telling. "The chemistry between us has been building up for a while." That's what Wyatt had told her to say, right? "It needed to be kissed out." How stupid did she sound right now?

"Uh-huh. Whatever." He rolled his eyes. "Now that you've both got all that hormonal mistakenness out of your systems, drop it, and let's get back to normal." Heath huffed through his nose. If he'd been a cartoon character, two separate white steam clouds would have shot out of it. "Did you hear me?"

"Loud and clear." *What level of embarrassment did this put Chelsea at— to be babysat about a kiss?* Probably a ten out of ten. Out of curiosity, though, she asked, "What did Wyatt tell you after you whaled on him?"

Heath's face darkened. "Never mind."

Oh, interesting. Chelsea's soul lightened. She'd just ask Wyatt himself. "Where is he, by the way?"

"If he knows what's best for himself, he went home."

A peek through the lace curtains showed Wyatt's car still sitting in the driveway.

"Why are you even here tonight, Heath?"

"I came down to practice with you guys, as a surprise, and then you weren't showing up right away so I asked Mom to fetch you, and the next thing I know I hear—from Esther Lang, of all people—that the two of you are macking on each other in the living room and I should go on in if I want a peep show."

Peep show! Well, if their kiss had been as hot to watch as it was to participate in, maybe that was an accurate description.

"You didn't let us know you were coming. You've been pretty unreliable lately, you'd better admit."

"Hey. Don't forget you're my little sister."

"Yep, and that's why I can tell you the truth. It's motivated by love and Christmas caring."

Heath muttered something under his breath about Christmas caring not being a real term. "Well, I'm here now, and we'll practice for our wedding performance in the morning before I have to go back tomorrow. It would have been better tonight."

"Except you sent Wyatt packing."

"Whatever. Somebody's got to protect you."

"From what? From Wyatt?"

"From ..." He didn't answer. "I'm just steamed, okay? We always said there would be no inter-trio dating."

"With you as my brother, that only left me and Wyatt with the edict. Why would you care?"

"It's about balance. When two in a singing group pair off, the team always fails. Look at Narcissa. Look at Great Scott. If you don't want to look beyond Sugarplum Falls, think of The Holly Jollies. They had a trio, two got together, and the whole thing fell apart. That's when Christmas Tree-O started, and we had to take all their singing gigs that first year. It was hard work. I swore I wouldn't let that happen to us."

But he *was* letting it happen by moving on in life. Heath was the one who'd found love, and he was moving forward. Shouldn't Wyatt and Chelsea be allowed to as well?

She said none of this. There was no arguing with him when he was worked up. Maybe tomorrow he'd cool down. Instead, all she said was, "Sometimes you're not very easy to get along with, Heath." And he was exhausting in that respect. *Maybe that's why I'm so drawn to Wyatt.* Wyatt could smooth over any rocky path, any prickly social situation, and make everyone calm down. Even Heath.

"Sometimes you do stuff that makes me hard to get along with."

"Your reactions are your own responsibility, my friend."

"I'm going to bed. We practice our songs for the rehearsal dinner and wedding at seven a.m." He marched toward the stairway.

What? They were singing not only at the rehearsal dinner tomorrow, but also at the actual wedding? Could Chelsea just melt into the floor now, please?

Chapter 12

Wyatt

Wyatt tapped an erratic rhythm on the steering wheel of his car. Surely Chelsea would come out soon. Her silhouette and Heath's shaded the front room curtains of Holly Berry House for a long time. Everything inside him wanted to jump out of the car and get in there and defend her, but logic reminded him he'd had enough of Heath and his lectures for the evening. And Heath had probably heard more than enough from Wyatt.

The truth was, getting between him and his sister wouldn't fly with the sister. Sutherland loyalty, and all that.

Unlike North loyalty.

If I'm going to keep dating—and kissing—Chelsea, the last thing I should do is drive a wedge deeper between myself and her brother, whether or not he's my best friend.

Preserve the relationship, so that he could create the relationship.

That's what he wanted to do, right? Totally yes when he was in the midst of that brain-melting, soul-soaring kiss with her. It had been a summation of desire of every other kiss he'd experienced in his life, and then expanded exponentially, like the Big Bang Theory, only for emotional creation, rather than the universe itself.

Except ... that kiss had felt like Wyatt's whole universe.

I really, really like this girl. I've never actually felt this way, not this strongly. Sure, it had come on fast, but it hadn't been a fast relationship. They'd been circling each other for ages, a lifetime, like planets caught in each other's gravity, and now suddenly nudged by some freak meteor impact—the Fargo wedding—so they crashed into one another. The problem was, Wyatt had no idea how to handle a *real* relationship. Everything up to now had felt disposable, awful as that must sound to anyone else. Maybe temporary was a better word. A time-filler until the real match for his soul appeared.

It might be Chelsea. It feels like it's Chelsea.

Heath's accusations had just rolled off Wyatt. Whatever. None of them were new. Some of the rebukes he deserved, of course—the well-trodden ground of date-all-the-cheerleaders was a classic. But some Wyatt didn't deserve, like the also well-worn rut of the girl's choice dance railing. Heath simply didn't have all the information on why Wyatt would ditch the first girl after saying yes and go with a second. No denying it had happened, but the why was what mattered.

Frankly, Heath even now believed Wyatt had done it because the second girl was cuter. Heath considered Wyatt a total jerk to women. What he didn't know was that the first girl had been handpicked by Mom and had only asked out Wyatt because Mom had paid her to. The girl got her money, which was what she'd wanted. Nor did Heath know that the second girl who asked him had been a math major, and she'd reminded Wyatt of Chelsea. He'd just been approximating the ideal.

And Wyatt hadn't shared the *why*. Until tonight.

It had taken, oh, five percent of the wind out of Heath's sails of fury.

But he'd still gone away mad.

Heath's temper could take days to cool off. Like a slow-release on a pressure cooker.

Wyatt could wait. Probably. At least, in the meantime he could refuse to let it get under his skin. Honestly, nothing could get too deep under his skin except that kiss of Chelsea's tonight.

Shazowie.

The front door opened, and Chelsea came out. In a flash, Wyatt was out of his car and at her side.

"Hey. Can I drive you home?"

"I live on the property, remember?"

"But it's cold outside."

"I really can't stay." She intoned it in the tune of the Christmas song. Wyatt's heart did a little flip.

"No need to go away." He sang back, changing the lyrics. "I'll hold your hand, so it's not like ice." He reached for it, and she didn't pull back. "Okay, enough of that song. Quick, think of a different one."

"Oh, the weather outside is frightful?" she sang.

"That works." It worked well, driving the other lyrics aside and replacing them with visions of cozy fireplaces and cuddling up.

They headed, walking, into the moonlit night toward where her cottage lay at the wooded edge of the property of Holly Berry House, their feet crunching on the snow, the air smelling like wood fires and evergreens. It was just like that song about walking in a winter wonderland.

"Heath," she said with a dragging sigh.

"Heath," Wyatt echoed, with a low growl of annoyance.

She kept her eyes ahead. "I can guess what he said to you. No need to repeat it, especially if threats to body parts or expletives are involved. What I want to know is what you said back."

They arrived at her front door. "Can I come in?"

She pulled out her house key. "I don't know, Wyatt. It's been quite a long day." When he held out her massive shopping bag full of boxes from Crossing Clothiers she accepted it. "Thanks for these, by the way."

"You'll stun them all. You'll make the bride look second tier." Easy, though. The bride *was* second tier. "I still want to answer your question—but with a question. Can I come in?"

Chelsea bit her lower lip in the way that she had when she'd been considering kissing him before. "It's late."

"Yeah." *And we could stay up even later, finishing what we started.* "Somehow I'm not tired." He pressed his advantage. "You don't look tired either, Chelsea. You look like you want to finish our conversation." And other things. "You're keeping me from playing my Scrabble word. I think you're trying to keep me from getting too far ahead."

His current slate of Scrabble letters appeared in his mind: *K-I-S-S H-E-R.* Okay, okay, if the letters insisted, how could Wyatt refuse?

He lowered his chin and gazed deeper into her eyes.

She moistened her lips and pressed open her door. "Okay, but let's talk."

Chapter 13

Chelsea

Chelsea took her coat and shopping bags to her bedroom, leaving Wyatt in the living room, and shutting the door behind her. Oh, when he'd stood on her doorstep, gazing at her so intently, it had been all she could do not to resume their earlier kiss. He was so near, and the doorstep was where she'd always imagined her first kiss with a date to be.

The one with Fargo—in the men's room at the university library—*don't ask*—absolutely didn't count as a first kiss. Nor should any subsequent kisses with Fargo, her first and last boyfriend.

But then again, neither should the situation-forced kiss in the front room at Holly Berry House with Wyatt.

No, the front stoop of Holly Berry Cottage, or even in front of the fireplace or the piano, was a much more romantic setting for a first kiss.

Not that she should be thinking about kissing him again, not after the hullabaloo of Heath's rage—and the fact she'd see her brother in the morning again.

She placed the dresses from Wyatt on hangers and held them up. The burgundy silk was everything. She held it to her chin, and swayed back and forth. *Wyatt chose it for me.*

And he'd announced they were engaged.

Hrrmmm.

"Hey, you ever coming out here again to see my Scrabble word or not?" Wyatt called. "And do you have anything to drink besides eggnog?" Yeah, because he despised nutmeg as much as he hated ginger.

"How many points, just tell me how many points. You can add them to the score card. I'll trust you this time." Not that he'd ever inflated his score. "There's lemon lime soda in the fridge."

"Only nine points." His voice had a nervous jitter—not Wyatt's usual style. The fridge opened with a creak and shut with a clunk. "But you'll want to see it."

Nine? Come on. "That's weak sauce." She had shed her jacket and shoes. Yeah, this sweater did hug her figure well—as evidenced by Fargo's stare earlier. Ooh, and Wyatt's right now.

"I like the sweater. The jeans, too."

"You bought it for me. The jeans I found in a forgotten box." Along with a few other things. *Why do I suddenly want to catch Wyatt's eye with form-fitting sweaters?* Oh, yeah. To get him to look at her like a hungry man right before a holiday feast, like he was right now. "Now, what's your word? Hey, what happened to our game?"

"I did mention it was a two-word word, right? I adjusted a few things."

"A few!" Every previously built word was messed up, the letters askew, missing, all of their builds pushed to the side in a heap, even her amazing word using both J and Z. "Not only did you wreck the board, you stole from my tray. I'm missing a letter D, which I needed for the word ..."

But her voice trailed off as he placed the letters one by one on the cleared center area of the game board, leaving the star starting space as the break between the two words he'd created.

*D-A-T-E * M-E*

Chelsea blinked at the little wooden tiles. They floated in a sea of gray and pink and blue squares, arranging and rearranging themselves until they finally smacked her with the full force of their import.

"Date you?" she whispered. "But ..."

"I know. You don't have to add the *but we're already engaged* part." He stepped into her personal space, shrinking it mightily. "We can let others believe we're engaged while the two of us share the secret that we're dating."

A secret. The idea of sharing a personal secret with Wyatt North made stars twinkle somewhere in Chelsea's chest.

"Engaged has escalated far past dating."

"What if I tell you I'll do it right?"

"Do what right?"

"Date you." Wyatt took a strand of her hair and pushed it off her neck, his fingers sliding over her skin and turning her insides to crystallized pink sugar. "Court you, if you want me to use an old-fashioned term."

Court her. "As in date-to-build-a-relationship?" Wyatt North didn't get into relationships. He kissed girls and then bowed a curt *sayonara* after taking what he wanted.

Just like Fargo Frye.

"I'm not sure, Wyatt."

"Would another kiss, just the two of us, with no one else around, help you sort out your decision?"

It might. It just might. "We'd have to try it to see, I guess."

Wyatt took Chelsea's hand and led her away from the Scrabble game. He pulled her across the room to the fireplace, where a blaze crackled and hissed. Apparently he'd been busy warming things up while she was in the back room.

"You know, Chelsea. Our other kiss can't really count as our first kiss."

"Oh?" Chelsea asked as he positioned her in front of the hearth, and its glow lit his features, making them warm, inviting, irresistible. "What makes you say that?" *What makes you able to read my mind?*

"That one was staged."

"Staged? As in planned ahead of time?" It most certainly had not been. When Chelsea kissed Wyatt he'd obviously been caught off guard.

"As in, for the benefit of an audience."

Oh, that kind of staged. Even though the audience—Fargo and Esther, and later Heath—had been unplanned. "You're saying you felt nothing." *Liar.*

"I'm saying, I'd like to give it another try. Without any spectators. Just ... you and me, Chelsea." He rested his forehead against hers, his breath soft against her lower lip. "Since we're dating now."

"We are?" Her knees wobbled.

"Uh-huh." With his nose, he pressed her face to tilt her chin upward, then brushed her lower lip with his own, and whispered, "Secretly."

She met his kiss, dissolving into it, like powder snow into saltwater. Instant. Complete. Irrevocable.

Wyatt North had often claimed he didn't do much math, but Chelsea was here to tell him, his kiss took her to all the mathematical places: algebraic equations, absolute values, the umpteenth decimal place of pi ...

She rode an undulating parabola in his kiss as it delved deeper and deeper into her fractional soul, spiraling her through Euclidian geometric shapes into a more whole vision of herself, and him, as the infinite—together.

Her breath came faster, and his hands slipped from her hips to the bare skin between her jeans and the hem of her sweater. Hot, rough-skinned, demanding, his hands pulled her to his torso, and she melted against him, and they were the fire, and ...

"Just a second, Wyatt." She heaved a breath and pushed him back. "I'm ... Whoa. What on earth was that?"

"Something only measurable by Richter and his scale, I'd say." His chest rose and fell. He wiped his brow with the back of his hand. "Chelsea." He went to the chintz armchair that faced the fire and fell into it, beckoning for her to join him in it.

"Wyatt. I'd better not. Being vertical in the last two kisses was ... yeah. Enough of a temptation." Additional physical contact and the potential for another kiss was just plain unwise.

Because being that close to him and *not* kissing him was a mathematical impossibility—a DNE *does not exist* result.

Chelsea took the other armchair. They shared the ottoman, both putting their feet up on it, her toes bumping against his wool socks.

"So far, dating you has been really rewarding." Wyatt batted her foot with his, then rested it solidly against hers. The contact wasn't traditionally romantic, but every touch from Wyatt felt like a continuation of what had gone before. "I don't care what Heath thinks. That's what I told him when he chewed me out—to answer your earlier question."

Finally. After much delicious ado, the answer had actually come. "You actually told him you don't care what he thinks? How did he react?" Not well, most likely.

"As you might expect."

"Did you tell him about Fargo and Esther and the whole reason we're doing what we're doing?" Even though it wasn't exactly the *whole reason* anymore. At least not for Chelsea. "How did he take that?"

"With Fargo and Esther possibly within earshot? Would I really do that?"

"Good call." *So how had he explained it, then?*

"For that reason, you can't care what he thinks, either. Not that you should anyway."

"What do you mean? Don't you think who you date should matter to your family?"

"Not necessarily." Wyatt frowned. "I mean, if they get along, that's great. But family approval can't be the sole reason for staying together, nor should disapproval be the sole reason for breaking up."

"I think that has to depend on the temperament of the family member in question," Chelsea said. There was Heath's volatile temper to consider—plus his overprotective streak. But there was also Wyatt's mom's whole *anti-Chelsea* vibe, plus her own mom's cryptic misgivings. "The sane ones' opinions should be given greater weight."

"Maybe." Wyatt frowned. "You're not saying you'd dump a guy over a family opinion, are you?"

"I mean, it matters. I do care about my family's opinion."

The air shifted. Maybe a draft came down the chimney and the fire flickered and cooled. Wyatt pulled his feet off the ottoman. "I'd better get going."

Yeah. Before Chelsea changed her mind about joining him in that other chair.

He shoved his shirttail back into his jeans. When had it come untucked? Oh, maybe during the math equation.

"Heath wants to practice tomorrow morning. Seven o'clock."

Wyatt didn't stop to turn around when he answered her. "Yeah, okay." His feet shoved into his boots, and he tugged his coat sleeves over his arms. "See you in the morning, then. Up at Holly Berry House."

Whoa. If Chelsea's neck joints had been designed differently, her head would be spinning at the speed with which Wyatt left. She pulled back the curtain, but he was already back at the big house and his car lights were disappearing down the driveway.

Did he just kiss me and diss me?

Uh-oh.

Nah. That was just her imagination. The heat between them was hotter than Caliente Cocoa with ten shakes of Tabasco sauce. It was lip-meltingly hot. Willpower-meltingly hot. In fact, she'd almost lost her darn mind in the heat of that kiss.

With steps lighter than air, Chelsea polkaed her way to the storage room of the cottage, braved the chill, and searched until she found the box labeled *Stuff I Don't Need.* She hauled it into the house. Curling iron. Straightening iron. Makeup from her days worrying about how she looked on stage as part of Christmas Tree-O. Jewelry of every level of chunkiness.

One by one, she placed the items in reach. *I used to be this person.* The person with a straight spine, with shoulders back and chin held high. A person who could laugh with others and lift them up—and not just by fixing their computers and phones when a virus or tech-mayhem struck. *I used to talk to people. Listen to their hearts. I've been so busy wallowing for the past year and a half, I've barely left my house, except for mandatory family events and service projects. I haven't reached out to anyone else for their needs.* And she certainly hadn't used any of the items in the neglected box of prettifiers.

Ooh, there was that deep-red lipstick she'd bought but never dared try. How would it look with the fitted black silk dress? She slathered it across her raw lips, and then lifted the man crusher dress to her front and stood in front of the mirror.

Yeah, this would do. *I'm not actually half bad in this.* And to think, it took Wyatt North, of all people, to blast her eyes back open about herself, instead of feeling like the ugly frump who was only good for math tutoring. Or cheating. Whatever. She was coming to life again!

Wyatt won't be able to look away.

But then again, neither would anyone else, once they saw her and Wyatt together, now that the Sutherland family rumor mill was likely grinding at full power about Wyatt's announcement.

How was Chelsea supposed to field those questions? They would not be few.

93

With Wyatt at her side, though, it should be fine. He was the one with all the social skills, the feather-un-ruffling abilities. Despite his recent penchant for exaggerating their relationship, she should definitely let him do the talking.

Unless he was still in whatever mood he took up as he raced out of here like he'd seen the hood and scythe of the Ghost of Christmas Yet to Come.

Chapter 14

Wyatt

It turned out, Wyatt was the one to skip the Christmas Tree-O practice this time. Of course, he had good reasons for it. North Star Capital always held early morning meetings of the executive board, and for the first time, Mom invited Wyatt.

"You're ready to present on your findings, I assume." She fell into lockstep beside him as they entered the firm's large door from the parking lot in the pre-dawn winter morning.

He was not. Too many other things had pushed to the forefront of his priorities. "I've done the research, but the numbers are not coming out clear to me yet. I want to be careful and get us the best return on investment possible." ROI was everything at North Star Capital.

Brace for impact.

Mom turned to face him, and they stopped just outside the doors to the conference room. "I can't tell you how glad I am to hear that."

Wait, what? "Oh?" He had to cough to mask the shock in his voice. "Why's that?"

Mom looked at her nails. "An investment opportunity has presented itself in exactly the amount you've been allotted. I'd like you to take a serious look at it."

"Sure." He'd do that. Especially since he knew the audience he was playing for—pleasing exactly two people: Mom and Dad. Mostly Mom. "Send me the information. Anything you want to tell me up front about it?"

"Yes, one thing—that it's not merely a monetary ROI we'd be looking at with this opportunity." That was new. "It would pay future networking dividends, and I believe would be good for the community."

"It sounds perfect." Especially if it was also tied to a local business.

Sugarplum Falls should take top billing in their investment priorities—even if Mom didn't always think so. "Any ties to Sugarplum Falls?"

"In fact, yes."

Hot diggity. "I'll study it thoroughly, but I'm getting a good feeling about it already." Much better than about that failing hospital or that real estate investment with wetlands concerns he'd investigated on the list he'd been handed earlier. "Thanks for the tip."

"I'm getting a great feeling about it, too." Mom hugged him. Whoa. It took a second to relax into the hug, but he got there. "It's great working with you side by side for all our futures, son. Yours, mine, Dad's, your someday-family's."

Before Mom could extrapolate the Someday-Family into some alliance between Wyatt and that Rowena Gustavson person, he escaped into the board room. There waited hot apple cider from The Cider Press and fresh apple doughnuts from Sugarbabies as his first ever taste of executive life. This was great.

Except for one big problem.

The discussion focused on a litany of complex financial numbers surrounding a project Wyatt hadn't been looped in on, so when his cider and doughnuts were gone, it was only Wyatt and his doodle pad.

And his toxic thoughts.

Chelsea. It matters to her what Heath thinks. Well, he's more on the crazy-so-we-downgrade-his-opinion's-weight side, but definitely about what Mrs. Sutherland thinks. What did Mrs. Sutherland think of Wyatt? She did treat him like a son. But when it came to Wyatt and Chelsea as an entity, her words from the hot cocoa tasting night were all he had to go on.

Wyatt North is the one you're seeing? Mrs. Sutherland had said that night in obvious disbelief. Or was it disdain? When she'd asked what had changed between Wyatt and her daughter, she'd definitely used cautious tones. Not exuberant ones. And there'd been no embrace, no *welcome to the Sutherland family* warm hug.

Either the woman was clairvoyant and could see through their ruse, or else she was highly protective of her daughter—and didn't trust Wyatt.

Wasn't Wyatt trustworthy as a boyfriend? Er, fiancé?

Maybe he shouldn't answer that, based on his well-known track record of dating and then ignoring girl after girl.

No wonder Mrs. Sutherland hadn't gushed over him with anything but skepticism. What did they call that? Karma? Payback? Getting your just desserts?

But the pure fact was that up to now, Wyatt hadn't dated any girl who'd motivated him to change his game. To stand taller. To be anything other than a good time with a bottomless bank account.

Does Chelsea even know about my bank account? Never once had his financial situation come up between them. Sutherlands in general seemed oblivious to financial status. Ike Sutherland, on a high school administrator's salary, had built up their patch of land on Holly Berry House, a place big and welcoming enough that it could draw in close or distant relatives as a spot for wedding celebrations, or host gatherings where scores of Sutherlands could sip cocoa and sing and laugh—and they didn't really care what anyone else had or didn't have.

They never made any comparisons.

Which is one of so many things that makes Holly Berry House home. Not a house, like North Forty, the name Mom had bequeathed her modern metal and glass structure on forty acres overlooking Sugarplum Falls. The best, only the best and latest and finest and newest design, at North Forty. Art, chrome, brushed nickel.

Doodles of stark rectangles and ice cubes filled his legal pad down one side. The other side slowly filled with images of fireplaces and music notes and Scrabble tiles and cups of cocoa.

Only ten hours until their date to the engagement party and more time with Chelsea. And maybe a chance to convince her that he wasn't the man her mom assumed him to be.

***

After dinner at Mario's, Wyatt pulled up at Holly Berry House, wedging his car among about fifty others. The Sutherlands always turned out en masse for family functions.

"You going to be all right?"

She should not be shaking. In that black dress from Gregor and Amélie, with the way her hair cascaded and her full-on red lipstick, she'd inspire fear, not reap it. *Esther should be scared. Chelsea might take her man's attention.*

"When we walk in there tonight, everyone is going to swarm us." Chelsea bit the knuckle of her index finger. "Are we ready for that?"

Wyatt was ready. What did he care? Swarms could be fun. "What's got you most nervous? Not the fact we're performing with Heath without practicing, I hope."

"Um, maybe the fact that we're supposedly engaged, and we're going to someone else's engagement party?"

Oh. That. "If people draw attention to us, just flash them your biggest smile, and then turn the conversation back to the guests of honor. You'll come across as magnanimous. It'll be a breeze."

"A breeze if I had your charm, maybe. Have you ever noticed how much of that I lack?"

In no universe did Chelsea lack charm. "I beg to differ. But if you like, I'll field the questions. You can refer them all to me. To make that happen, though, you'll have to stick right close to my side all night." Definitely not a bad prospect, as long as she didn't tell him she cared more about her brother Heath's opinion and her mom's than about their potential relationship. *Their relationship which could be a very good thing.*

Wyatt helped her out of the car, and slipped her hand through the crook of his arm. As they climbed the steps to the well-lit front porch bedecked with a lit Christmas tree on either side of the entrance, the front door flew open, and out dashed Heath's wife Odessa, a hand on her very pregnant stomach.

"Chelsea! Oh, my gosh!" She air-kissed them as she dashed past. "You look gorgeous. Is that really you? I'm in a mess of a hurry right now to get to the store before they close. I'm out of prenatal vitamins, and I know I'll hate myself if I can't take one tomorrow morning. Don't want our little girl to miss out on a single IQ point, you know?"

"Can't Heath go for you?" Chelsea voiced Wyatt's question. The woman looked like her water could break any second.

"I like to choose the brand. It's fine." Odessa kept chugging down the walkway toward the parking area. "I'll only be gone two shakes of the cinnamon-sugar shaker, and when I get back I can't wait for you to show me your ring! I'll bet whatever rock Wyatt North gave you has major sparkle!"

Odessa's car lights came on and she pulled away.

Chelsea froze like she'd been hit with some kind of stun gun.

"Are you all right?" Wyatt asked, when Chelsea rooted herself to the porch boards and wouldn't go inside. "What's wrong?"

"Ring." Chelsea placed her right hand over her left.

"Oh." There would be questions. Not just from Odessa.

Getting questions about their engagement was bad enough—and it was Wyatt's fault that it was even coming up. His idea. His problem. Luckily, he had a very easy fix.

"Come with me." He took her hand, and they headed back to the car.

Seven minutes later, Wyatt pulled Chelsea into the foyer of North Forty. Brrr. Had Mom and Dad turned off the heat in here, since they never spent much time at home? And was Chelsea ever going to snap out of this conversation coma? She hadn't said anything except the word *ring* in the last ten minutes. He took her into the kitchen and planted her at the counter of the island.

"Mom? Dad? It's me. I'm just getting something from the storage closet." Wyatt headed for the staircase, but Mom whooshed around the corner from the den. "What's going on? No Christmas tree up yet? It's December, people. Time to celebrate the season," he hollered into the void.

Or so he thought.

"Wyatt, darling. I'm so glad you're here." So cool, so collected. "I wasn't expecting you, but I have—oh. The Sutherland girl is here, too." Her voice went from cool to icy. "I thought we'd discussed this."

Wyatt turned to Chelsea. "Will you be all right for a minute while I go get something?"

He should have checked ahead, verified the coast was clear—or left Chelsea in the car where it was safe. "I'll be right back." Before she could even nod, Wyatt was up the stairs and digging through a box in the storage closet on the landing of the upper floor. A-ha! Perfect. Beyond perfect.

But he'd been too slow. As he descended the stairs, stomping, taking three at a time back to the kitchen, Mom had already launched her attack.

"Chelsea, darling. You are certainly stepping things up tonight. Please say you're not upping your appearance game in an effort to snare Wyatt. The North family is really not ready for a Sutherland invasion. Keep in mind, the North beat the South."

Was she referencing the American Civil War? Who in Sugarplum Falls was at war? No one—except maybe Mom.

"Hey, Mom. What are you two talking about?" Wyatt gripped the ring in his palm. "Doesn't Chelsea look great for the engagement party?"

Mom's face turned to stone. "Engagement."

Chelsea held up a placating hand. "Oh, Mrs. North. It's for my cousin Esther and—"

Wyatt stepped between Chelsea and Mom. "Chelsea, let's not pretend. Not in front of my mom." He turned to face her, dropped to one knee, and opened his palm. "Chelsea, will you wear this ring?"

Chapter 15

Chelsea

Sparkling in the center of Wyatt's palm was the largest diamond Chelsea had ever laid eyes on, outside of the gem and mineral exhibit at the Sugarplum Falls Natural History Museum. All her physiological systems stopped, or maybe started running backward.

"Will you wear this ring?" Wyatt's words came down some sort of long tube, echoing from afar off. "Chelsea?"

The walls swayed. She grabbed onto the slate countertop of Mrs. North's massive kitchen island to steady herself, its chill seeping into her hand and up her arm. It grounded her but only partially. The rest of her soul had shot through a time machine to the night Fargo dumped her.

You can't be serious, Chelsea. You thought I *was going to offer you a ring? Ha, you? Please. What, like a big diamond of some kind? Seriously?* His laughter grated against her eardrums even now. *You, a diamond. Trust me, you're not the type of girl a guy thinks* diamond *when he sees her.*

Her stomach hurt, as if it was being twisted like a wet rag. "Wyatt, I can't—"

"That's *exactly* right!" Drusilla North flew at them, reaching for Wyatt's open palm, although he closed it in time to keep her from snatching the diamond ring. "What on earth are you thinking, son? My mother's diamond? For *her*?"

Exactly. Mrs. North nailed it. Chelsea stepped away from him, the sharp edge of the countertop knifing her in the back. Fight or flight? Definitely flight.

"Chelsea, wait." Wyatt reached for her hand, but she pulled it away. "My mother is being terrible right now."

No kidding. Truly terrible, and a harsh mirror of Fargo's treatment of Chelsea a year and a half ago, right after he found out he'd been admitted to the MBA program at that fancy school—thanks solely to Chelsea's tutoring him out of his failing grade in statistics.

"Chelsea, talk to me." Wyatt sounded desperate. "Please."

She couldn't talk, not for a long moment, but finally it came out in a thin mutter. "I'm not the kind of girl who gets diamonds. Certainly not like that diamond."

Mrs. North loomed up. "Listen to the girl, Wyatt. She makes sense, even if she is a Sutherland."

Wyatt pounded a fist on the countertop. "Mother! What in the world is with you and the Sutherlands? You've done nothing but insult Chelsea since she arrived, and you drove Heath out of here anytime he showed up, which meant I went to his house to hang out, which meant you drove me, your own son, out of your home based on—what? What is your problem?"

Chelsea steadied herself. This fight didn't belong to her, and she shouldn't hear it, even if it affected her. Greatly.

Willing her ankles to be strong in these ridiculous heels, she stepped out of the kitchen, through the cold foyer, and headed back out to Wyatt's car.

It was locked.

She stood at the door of the car. Through the window, on the seat, sat her phone.

I can't even call for a ride share. If North Forty weren't clear on the other side of Sugarplum Falls, Chelsea would have walked back to Holly Berry House, no matter how sharp the temperature drop.

But the high heels, the distance, the wind chill factor—she couldn't, *shouldn't*, after computing the mathematical odds of her snapping an ankle or catching pneumonia. Or at least getting frostbite.

She looked up at the stars. The holiday pop song for tonight's performance plinked through her brain. *"All I Want for Christmas is You."* It was Esther's request, and Heath, being Heath, hadn't said no—to either the special request or to the singing engagement in the first place. Didn't her own brother know the bad blood between Chelsea and Esther?

A dozen incidents flashed from times gone by—as if they were timed to the music just like the light show at Waterfall Lights.

The singer doesn't want a lot for Christmas. Ah, yes. There was the year as kids when Esther and Chelsea were on the same soccer team. Esther had played forward or defender in every game while Chelsea sat on the bench and handed out the juice boxes at the end—which wouldn't have bothered her, but Esther had gloated over it.

Not even snow. And could Chelsea forget the spelling bee, when Esther had won for the whole school on the word *poison*, after Chelsea flubbed the word *mistletoe*? Esther's taunt, *Chelsea will never have to worry about spelling it right. It's not like she'll ever be kissed beneath mistletoe anyway.*

All she wanted for Christmas was her true love. Yeah, Esther had ended up flirting relentlessly with any guy—seriously, *any* guy—who showed faint interest in Chelsea from the time they were old enough to notice boys. No guy had ever resisted Esther, either. Long blonde hair, flouncy walk, cheerleader. Even the captain of the Mathletes had fallen for her, temporarily, when she'd flirted outrageously with him. Of course, he ended up too scared to talk to girls after Esther had burned him so badly.

Sure, Esther and Fargo deserved each other, but still. It didn't feel great as a mocked onlooker.

Chelsea started to shiver uncontrollably.

Why did Esther always have to be such a jerk to Chelsea? Aunt Lisa and Uncle Sheldon were wonderful. Complete favorites. What had happened to their daughter sometime around the age of thirteen to make her such a rotten person? *We were friends before that. Close friends.*

A slam came from the house. Wyatt stomped through the snow toward Chelsea.

"You're still here." He clicked his key fob to unlock. "Let's go." He pressed her into her seat, but he didn't close the door. "Heath texted. We're up in ten minutes, and it's a seven-minute drive."

Oh. The performance. Chelsea winced.

"Can you do it?"

She swallowed and closed her eyes, nodding faintly. "The show must go on." For Aunt Lisa's sake, if not for Esther's. *I love Aunt Lisa. I love my whole extended Sutherland family. I'm not going to let them down.*

Coincidentally but unsurprisingly, the car radio played their performance song when Wyatt turned on the car. Chelsea resisted the urge to slap it off. When Wyatt pulled back into the parking area at Holly Berry House, the clock on the dashboard flashed eight o'clock. *Showtime.* Again with the rag-twisty stomach.

"Before we go in, Chelsea ..."

Oh, no. Here it came again. She clenched every muscle so hard it made her brain hurt.

"What are you going to say when Odessa asks to see your ring?" When all Chelsea did was squeeze her left hand's fingers with her right, Wyatt prodded further. "I'm really sorry. I shouldn't have done that back there. Not in front of my mom. Not when she was being such a pill."

"That's one word for her." Apparently her vocal cords had finally un-paralyzed themselves—just in time to sing, too. "You don't want to give me your grandma's diamond to wear."

"It's the only diamond I have access to for now. We're either doing this or we aren't. If you want, I can go in there and un-tell everyone the lie—before we perform, even. It's up to you."

That would definitely not make things better. But Wyatt also hadn't said he wanted to give her a diamond. *Remember, it's a ruse. It's not real. Quit letting yourself think otherwise.* "No."

"Fine, then. Let's just walk in there, heads held high, and smile, sing, and leave."

That wouldn't work, either. Aunt Lisa wouldn't stand for it. Neither would Aunt Rita, or Mom or Dad or Heath and Odessa or anyone. It was a full-on Sutherland minefield, and Chelsea was going to have to navigate it.

"Give me that." She held out her hand. "Just ... put it on me. I'll try to keep it from getting dirty or whatever."

"Chelsea, what's going on? Don't you like the ring?"

She froze again.

"If it's way too old-fashioned, we can just tell Odessa and everyone else that your ring is getting sized. I'll get you something much better from Bijoux Jewelry first thing Monday morning. I know the ring is old. The diamond isn't the type that everyone wants these days."

Chelsea's voice shrank, as if she were a Who down in Whoville. "The ring is perfect. It's gorgeous."

"Then I don't understand. Help me out here, Chelsea." He pulled back. "If it's me, and if you think your family won't approve and you're concerned about what they'll think of you for being with me, then ..."

Oh, no! It wasn't that! "Give that to me." She whipped it out of his hand and shoved it onto her ring finger. *It's a perfect fit. Oh, and look how it picks up the light of even the faintest glow of his dashboard. The fire of this diamond!* She didn't deserve it. But she also couldn't let Wyatt think she had a problem with *him.* "Let's go in."

Wyatt sprang from the driver's side, and soon they were inside, where Heath already stood in front of the hearth in the front room, as if ready to offer a solo in case Wyatt and Chelsea didn't show. The piano had been rolled in from its spot beneath the grand staircase, and provided a focal point for the gathered crowd, which included everyone from Aunt Lisa and Uncle Sheldon, to cousins and second cousins like Mack and his wife, to Kaden and Jaidyn in elf hats, to the guests Chelsea had little desire to honor—Fargo and Esther.

Everyone's eyes were on Chelsea and Wyatt, especially Heath's. Which were furious.

"Finally. You've been, what? Making out?" Heath said under his breath. "You guys are so dead." It made Chelsea's fragile spirits even more brittle.

"Back off, Heath." Wyatt pushed his shoulder. "Now's not the time."

Yeah. Exactly. *He just told Heath to cool it.* Whoa. That calmed Chelsea's nerves. She twisted the ring a few times. She could do this. Wyatt was with her.

Standing in the front row of the circled-up crowd, Fargo and Esther reigned for the moment. But while Fargo's gaze should have been adoringly glued to Esther at his side, instead, it was trained on Chelsea.

And it looked ravenous as it crawled up and down Chelsea's new dress, pausing at strategic points. He gave her an appreciative leer.

Maybe I shouldn't have dared wear the red lipstick. Drusilla North certainly hadn't done anything but frown at Chelsea for it—that, and accuse her of trying to hook Wyatt, and uncivilly declare herself at war with Chelsea's family.

"I'll talk to you in a minute," Heath growled at Wyatt.

Heath clapped for everyone to be quiet. "Now that Wyatt and Chelsea are here, everyone listen up as Christmas Tree-O performs Esther's romantic holiday request. We dedicate to the happy couple, 'All I Want for Christmas Is You.'" He played a couple of chords on the piano, and they all found their note for the a cappella number. "One, two, a-one-two-three-four."

Heath took the lead, singing lines like just wanting someone for his own, and Chelsea chimed in with Wyatt on all the oohs and ahhs. The song was much more a solo with backup singers than a trio type of performance. Which probably suited Heath perfectly—and it fit Chelsea's mood of the moment.

The song ended, and everyone clapped. Heath took Wyatt practically by the ear and dragged him out of the family room, leaving Chelsea to the wolves.

"Guys?" But they were gone.

Thanks, guys. Just when she needed Wyatt most! And he'd promised to answer any and all questions about the engagement. *No wonder Mom said he wasn't reliable.*

Of course, Heath had more to do with this abandonment than Wyatt.

The ring on her finger was like holding a barbell. With huge effort, she lifted her hand to push stray hair from her face, and in the front row, Esther gasped, her eyes on the ring.

"Will you look at that?" Esther murmured. When Aunt Lisa shot Esther a *shush it, baby,* look, Esther covered with, "Where on earth did you get that cubic zirconium? It's the size of ... Fargo's wisdom tooth."

Gross.

Odessa to the almost-rescue. "Oh, sweetie! Now that we're in the light, I'm just astounded by how gorgeous it is. I'm sure you spend half your days just a-staring at it, don't you?" Odessa had one of those accents no one could resist. "Let me be the first to take a real look at it tonight."

No one would push a pregnant woman aside, so Odessa got her look-see, and Esther vocally excused herself to get something to drink. Others left the dining room for the buffet in the kitchen.

Meanwhile, Fargo's stare took its own lingering meander over Chelsea's body again. "Looking good, Chelse. Real good." He popped his tongue against the side of his mouth as if he was from one of those New York City boroughs where women took that sound as a compliment.

Odessa side-hugged Chelsea with a dense flurry of congratulations and then got distracted by a tray of shrimp cocktail, leaving Chelsea alone with a ravenous-looking Fargo.

"Why'd you never sexy it up like this for me? When *we* were dating?"

He thought she looked sexy?

"Looking at you tonight, it feels like I owe you a huge apology."

"For what, exactly?"

This is the moment I craved. This is exactly what I told Wyatt I wanted.

"For overlooking so many of your finer details. I was young, what can I say? And stupid."

That was not up for debate. "Apology accepted."

"Does that mean"—he leaned in and placed his lips much too close to her ear, whispering and putting Chelsea into a time warp back to when she'd thought he was everything—"that maybe you and I could get some alone time to discuss old times? Maybe, say, around midnight? I hear you live in the cottage out back. I'll be there. Answer when I knock three times."

Chapter 16

Wyatt

“**M**r. Sutherland, sir.” Wyatt's shoes were suddenly a size too small there in Chelsea's dad's presence.

“Sir, is it now?” Mr. Sutherland laughed a big gut-laugh that filled the entire den. A log burning in the hearth dropped, shooting out sparks, probably due to the sound concussion from Chelsea's dad's big laugh. “Why couldn't I get you to call me that when you were sent to my office as your principal? It was always Ike then.”

“I'm so sorry about that, sir. I had some growing up to do back then.”

Mr. Sutherland—Ike—raised one of those eyebrows that said *only back then? What about now, too?* But there was nothing believable or convincing Wyatt could offer in the moment. His changes had been too recent to show any kind of track record. *I know for myself how the past weeks have changed me from a guy who shows very little promise to a guy with a mission in both career and relationship goals, but how can I possibly convey that to him without sounding braggy about potentially becoming vice president at North Star, or without boasting that Chelsea and I are in love and I can possibly, eventually, be worthy of her?* Ike wouldn't believe him any more than Heath had.

“Go eat rocks,” Heath had said ten minutes ago. “And hands off my sister.”

When Wyatt had mentioned that Heath was wrong about Wyatt's past, Heath muttered something like, *Fine, but that doesn't mean I have to like it yet.*

But Chelsea is the one whose opinion matters here, Wyatt had argued.

I thought we had an understanding. No dating.

We're not dating. We're engaged.

Heath had just made a fist and pounded it on a piece of paper on the table.

Then he'd picked up a pencil and written the words *your face* on the paper and stormed out with an *I'll have to think about this.*

That was when Ike had walked in and invited Wyatt to his book-filled den.

Now, there he stood. Which would be better? Getting his face beaten in by Heath, or this?

The face beating. Hundred percent.

"I know you must think the relationship between Chelsea and me looks sudden." And fake, probably. Ike wasn't stupid. He'd likely seen hundreds if not thousands of fake, juvenile excuses for behavior in his career. "I'd like to tell you it isn't."

Except he couldn't. Because it would be a lie—sort of. *It's been brewing. But the stove got turned off, and then back on again, the second we started playing this game.* It didn't feel like a game anymore. Not after tonight, not after what he'd said to his mother. Defending Chelsea to Mom had solidified something inside him. And it was a good thing Chelsea had been out of earshot, or she'd be more than freaking out about wearing that ring right now.

"Wyatt," Ike said, motioning for him to take a chair. The fire crackled again. "I'm going to tell you what my problem with this situation is."

Uh-oh. Here it comes again. *Wyatt North is a goof-off. Not reliable. Not good enough for our brilliant, talented, shooting-star of a daughter.* Or sister, or niece. Or whatever. Didn't matter which Sutherland relationship, they all had to believe that about Chelsea's being out of Wyatt's league.

"Sir, I know I haven't always looked like a young man of promise." Despite his connections to North Star Capital, which a lot of families in town might consider promising, the Sutherlands wouldn't be fooled by that smokescreen to a man's character. "But if you'll listen for a minute, I can explain."

Could he? Could Wyatt reveal their ruse to Chelsea's dad—humiliating her even further? Or without insulting Ike Sutherland?

Decidedly not.

"What I mean to say is—"

"Wyatt, stop," Ike roared. "You didn't listen to what I had to say before you jumped in with your litany of excuses, which I didn't ask for and don't need."

He didn't need them? "I'm sorry, sir. Excuse me for interrupting." Wyatt sat up straighter. This was not his finest hour in front of Mr. Sutherland, and he'd had a few doozies. However, Ike's tone wasn't as irritated as the words themselves might have appeared. Instead, he wore a half-smile, like the whole thing was an inside joke Wyatt was missing.

"You don't need to explain. Of all people, *I* know Chelsea is a girl worth scooping up the second you can get her to say yes to a proposal, and waiting even the ten minutes necessary to ask her father's permission first would seem like a risky move."

Father's permission.

Ohhhhhhh. So that's what this was about.

"If I've offended you, sir. I—"

"Offended me!" Ike did have an ear-splitting roar. "Some young man who I've loved like a second son for a decade tells me he wants to make himself legally my son, and you think that offends me?"

It had been many years since Wyatt had suffered from tremors in his knees when things got tricky emotionally for him. Probably not since one of their first few concerts when they became Christmas Tree-O and he'd been expected to hit some kind of high note on "O Holy Night" before Heath commandeered all melody parts.

But he was shaking now. Big time.

I never once thought I'd be looking at Ike and potentially setting him up to hurt him in any way.

"So, kiddo? What'll it be? Are you going to ask it outright like a man so I can yank you into a man-hug, or what?"

110

Chapter 17

Chelsea

F argo had somehow physically maneuvered Chelsea out of the family room, away from the hearth and piano, and into the nook along the loggia leading to the garage.

Out of everyone's sight.

Out of everyone's earshot.

"Fargo!" She shoved his arm from where it had slid around her waist, and his other arm from her shoulders. "Get off."

"Chelsea, baby." He snaked his arms around her again.

"Fargo, so help me, I will holler and Esther will come in here so fast. She's a hairdresser and very good with scissors." She tried, and failed, to untangle herself.

"You're very good with what you do, too. You make all the numbers add up." He pressed her closer.

"If you don't respect Esther enough to knock it off, at least I do." Finally, Chelsea extracted herself from his octopus hold and held him at bay. "What are you even thinking, pal? This is your engagement party to the woman you proposed to, gave a diamond to." *A woman who apparently deserved your diamond, unlike me.*

"That wasn't a diamond." A scoff the size of the Sugarplum Falls town Christmas tree fell from Fargo's mouth. "Are you kidding me right now? The size of rock she's wearing, if it were real, would cost more than I'm trying to raise for my new startup."

It wasn't real? "Does Esther know that?"

"CZs have more fire than natural diamonds. Besides, Esther just wants something to flaunt, so she'd never care."

So she didn't know. *And Fargo didn't consider Esther the type of girl who deserved a diamond either.*

Or, did he just not consider diamonds to be all that symbolic of a woman's value?

Chelsea's head spun, tilting her onto her side and then upright again.

He lunged for her again. "You're just so ravishing tonight. You're giving me a sweet tooth. Remember when we used to date a couple years ago?"

She dodged. "You mean when I used to tutor you in your statistics and business calculus classes and you referred to me as your girlfriend, but only when we were together? Because if that's dating, I do remember. Also, I recall that when I wasn't around, you mocked me. Yeah, those were good times."

"I was young. Foolish. Now I can see the huge mistake I made."

"Please leave me alone."

But he came at her again. "In that dress, how could you think you'd be alone for a second tonight?"

"You were using me back then, Fargo." Just like all the other jocks or student body officers or popular guys who'd hit on her from junior high on. They'd all only wanted her to do their homework for them, and then dump her. Except, the difference was, Fargo had been so expert she hadn't been able to see through his façade. He'd made her believe he was sincere.

"Oh, Chelse. You were using me right back. Admit it." He gave her one of those leering once-overs.

"In what universe could that be accurate?"

"In the universe where you wanted a hot athlete as a boyfriend to brag about to your friends."

What friends? "No member of the mathematics department at Darlington State knew who a single member of the basketball team was." Trust her on that. "I wouldn't have known who you were myself, if you hadn't singled me out." And torpedoed her self-confidence.

"You loved it, and you know it."

She had, at the time. Until he'd ripped her to shreds. "The second you got into your MBA program, you treated me like I was made of social poison. What would make you think I'd ignore that now?"

"Because you miss me, baby. Why else would you be wearing this, other

112

than to catch my eye? And the lipstick, baby, I can see now I was missing out on a much better time than I realized." His eyes crawled over her body like worms. Probably left slime trails, too. "Speaking of forgetting, don't think I haven't forgotten your hot kiss."

"Funny, I've completely forgotten yours." Finally, she gave a huge shove and extracted herself from his grasp. "Oh, Esther. Hi there."

Esther wasn't really there, but the feint did the trick, making Fargo spring back and gasp.

Chelsea made a dash for the living room and people and safety. Still no Wyatt, though. Where had he gone?

Instead, she met the glowering scowl of Heath, standing with his back to the fire, pacing.

"Why, you little ..." He didn't fill in the blank, but Chelsea could, with the name of the reindeer that paired with Prancer. "Flirting with my best friend not enough for you?"

Molten lead filled her stomach, spilling down into her lower limbs. "Heath, I—" It looked bad, really bad, and if he hadn't heard anything she'd said as she chewed out Fargo, then it looked even worse.

I got what I told Wyatt I wanted out of this fake relationship. All it had done was make her sick to her stomach, and choking on shame. *I should have left well enough alone.*

"Aw, come here, sis." Heath extended his arms. "Come on." It was like he really meant it. Was he planning to act eleven again and pin her arms to her side until she admitted wrongdoing?

She relented, and ... Heath actually hugged her. He hadn't been reprimanding her about that scene in the loggia with Fargo, after all. In fact, he patted the back of her head.

"Chelsea, I'm sorry."

Whoa. Two apologies in the same half hour? What was this, Christmas? *Almost.* "For what?"

"For being such a jerk to you about Wyatt."

What on earth? She pulled away. "I'm not following."

He held up both palms. "Hey, if you don't think I was being a jerk, fine.

113

I'll rescind my apology. Heck knows it was hard enough to offer."

"No, no. I accept. It's just—" Just what exactly did it mean? "Wyatt is really not a bad guy. He's been the best lately, actually." Helping Chelsea along the bumpy road of this awful Fargo and Esther situation, for instance. And bringing her dinner. And buying her clothes. And giving her a diamond. *A real diamond.* She looked down at her hand. Yeah, that was no substitute. It was an old mine-cut diamond, like they showed on those TV shows about antiques, and it had to be at least two carats. Maybe three.

Making me feel lovable.

"First off, I heard that Wyatt wasn't quite as big of a weasel in college as I thought." He sighed and rolled his eyes. "And that his big *sin* that I'd always attributed to him—which kept me from wanting him to date you, mainly—was kind of my fault."

"Your fault?"

"I mean, no. Not really. I ... Look, this isn't natural to me. Just accept that I was wrong and let's move on."

"Good enough." Sort of. "But, could you just give me a hint of how something sorta-sinful that Wyatt did could've been your fault? Just an inkling?"

Heath glowered. "I told him not to date you, and when he got a chance to date someone very similar to you, he jumped at it. Of course, the girl ended up being nothing like you, but ... yeah. He's liked you for a long time."

Me! "You mean—?"

"I mean it's a good thing I stood between the two of you up to now so that you could fall for him at precisely the right moment in life."

Ha. According to Heath's reckoning. But there was no reason to be peevish when he was doing his best. "Thanks, Heath. That means a lot."

Heath aimed a thumb toward the loggia to the garage. "I heard what you said to Fargo in there."

Chelsea's hand dropped to her leg, whacking her thigh hard.

"Why didn't you ever tell me what he did to you?"

Because you'd get blood on your hands? "I couldn't. But ... it's enough to say he wasn't kind to me—then or now."

114

"I knew that much, but I didn't know details." Heath put his arm around her shoulder. "Why didn't you tell me about Fargo's jerkitude back when it was going on? I would have pounded him into flour for you."

Exactly. "Because you would have pounded him into flour?" Hello. "You're a fighter not a lover, Heath."

"Tell that to Odessa."

"Historically," she amended. "So, I don't really want to look backward."

"No. I can understand that. Especially now that Fargo is going to be part of the family."

Ew. Did they really have to think of it that way? "They'll live in Caldwell City, where Esther will be doing celebrity hairstyles and Fargo will be running his fabulous new startup." Whatever that was. "I'll probably never have to see them. Who sees their cousins when they're adults, anyway?"

"Sutherlands."

Why did that have to be so true? So there was no escaping seeing Esther or Fargo. *Tonight's incident could rest heavy between us for a long time.* Although Fargo was still the villain, at least part of it was Chelsea's fault for the harebrained plan to make him jealous or sorry or … want her.

She shoved the heels of her hands into her eyes. "I'm pretty stupid sometimes."

"For a math genius, you sure are." Heath put an arm over her shoulder and jostled her. "But not stupid in choosing whose ring to accept."

Uh, what? Chelsea pulled back, more or less stuttering her question. "What are you saying?"

"I'm saying, you and Wyatt."

"What about us?" *Didn't Wyatt tell Heath about the fake-out? And now Heath isn't mad?* "I know it's crazy of us. And we probably shouldn't have done it at all."

"No, no. It's fine. It's great, actually."

Um, had Heath even *seen* the scary, overly effective, Fargo-mauling-Chelsea results of her and Wyatt's ruse? The fake relationship turned fake engagement couldn't be termed anything *but* stupid. "What part are you saying is great?"

In walked Dad. "Ho, there. My two beautiful children." He pulled Chelsea into one of his bear hugs. "I'm so glad to see you together and happy. And here's the young man who is tying it all together." He released Chelsea and tugged Wyatt next to his massive side, slapping him hard on the rib cage. "Wyatt, my future son-in-law, are you going to give Chelsea the good news, or should I?" He grinned so wide it showed his back teeth. "Oh, I will. Chelsea, in case you were worried, I did give Wyatt my permission."

Permission. For ... ?

Oh. *Ohhhh.* "Um, thanks, Dad." She met Wyatt's gaze. Yeah, there was an apologetic wince crinkling the sides of his eyes.

"I approve, too, in case anyone cares." Heath lifted his index finger in the air.

"You do?" Chelsea and Wyatt said at the same time, begging for a *jinx!* So that was what Heath meant by saying he thought it was great? *Our engagement is what he thinks is great?*

Dad and Heath high-fived, then set off for the buffet that was set up in the kitchen.

Chelsea backed up, banging her legs against the hearth, and then fell on her bottom onto the brick. The fire warmed her back, but it didn't thaw the shock that iced her soul. "Did that just happen?" She looked up at Wyatt.

He nodded. "I think so." He sat down beside her, taking her hand and inspecting it. He twisted the ring slightly to center it on her finger. "Unless this is all a very detailed dream. Let's just say if a clown walks through the room next with a plateful of bright green bunny rabbits singing 'I Saw Mommy Kissing Santa Claus,' we'll declare it a dream."

No clown appeared. Uncle Lester, however, scooted through humming "Jingle Bells" and eating handfuls of Mom's candy. "Uncle Lester didn't have bunnies. He doesn't count."

"Then this must be real."

Which meant Dad's and Heath's approval were real.

And she and Wyatt were pretty big jerks. *Unless it really was real.* Was it?

116

Chapter 18

Wyatt

Wyatt placed her left hand softly on her leg to view it, and then he put an arm around her waist to shield her back from the heat of the fire. The ring looked perfect on her finger.

It's getting too real. Which made him unstoppably talkative, apparently. "As a kid, I always wondered what it would be like to be part of the Sutherland family."

"You did?" Chelsea chuckled. "What did you think it would be like? Noisy, chaotic, with too much food and music and a hundred little kids running around getting underfoot?"

"More or less, but in all the good ways." In all the ways he thought would fill his soul starved for any kind of interactions that didn't involve numerical values. "It was warmer here."

"Do your parents even use the central heating in their house?" She curled her fingers, making the ring stand up even higher on her hand. "It was freezing in there tonight."

Yeah, for lots of reasons.

Wyatt gazed at the symbol of their commitment. "What's happening here, Chelsea?"

"I'm not exactly sure." She shook her head, and strands of her hair brushed against his cheek. "I mean, I want to remember that it's all just a put-on, a show."

"Uh-huh." Same with Wyatt. "But are you like me? Is it getting harder to distinguish the show from the reality?"

Chelsea rested her head on his shoulder. "I feel like someone is going to be really disappointed when this ends."

Yeah. Me. He didn't tell her about his argument with Mom—nor the point when he'd announced he was in love with Chelsea.

Instead, he told Chelsea about his meeting with Ike. She laughed. Then she told him about her run-in with Fargo.

"I'll channel my inner Heath and clean his clock."

"No need. I imagine word will somehow magically get back to Esther, since the house is small, and there was a lot of foot traffic. Then that clock of his will be so shiny clean it will double as a mirror for his conscience."

Good point. "What exactly did my mother say to you when I was upstairs getting my grandmother's ring?"

"It's your grandmother's?"

"From her marriage to her first husband, not my grandpa. He was a gold miner in the early days of settlement in Sugarplum Falls. She loved him, but he died in an accident. His mine shaft collapsed. She remarried my grandfather a few years later, but she always hung onto this ring as a symbol of her first love."

"Did that bother your grandpa?"

"He got the girl, he always said. If not her whole heart, he got her for his whole life, so he considered that a fair trade. He referred to her first husband as *the placeholder*—like that he'd kept her occupied until my grandpa could move out to this area and find Grandma."

"That's a bittersweet story." Chelsea held the ring up and tilted her hand back and forth. A passel of kids rushed through the room, sword fighting with empty wrapping paper tubes. "I'll give this back to you when we're done. Then your mom won't, you know, come after me in my sleep someday."

"So ..." Wyatt hadn't told Chelsea. "That's not going to happen."

"It's not?"

It wasn't. Not after the conversation Wyatt had had with Mom in the kitchen. "Trust me."

"Uh, I'll trust. But I'm going to tie up my camel by locking my doors and windows at night, just in case." Chelsea smiled.

"I can't blame you." Despite, the knock-down drag-out discussion, Wyatt still hadn't gotten to the bottom of Mom's disdain for Chelsea and her whole clan. Well, she'd just have to get over it soon, since Wyatt was going to be

118

joining the Sutherlands, becoming one of them.

Er, wait.

No, he wasn't.

This was fake.

Was it? Is it? Does it have to be?

"Let me walk you home." He helped Chelsea to her feet, and with coats on and scarves in place, they headed out the back door across Holly Berry House property to her cottage. "You've had a big day, you know. Getting a huge payoff for your efforts."

"Honestly, I could have done without that particular payoff. I guess we get what we thought we wanted sometimes, and then it's nothing like we expected. Be careful what you wish for, they say."

Probably so. Fargo and his grime ... "At least now you'll have no regrets."

"True. That's a good payoff." She reached over and took his mitten in hers. The night air turned their breath to white steam, glowing in the moonlight. Sounds from the party punctuated the air now and then, but they waned as Wyatt and Chelsea crunched over the gravel farther from the house.

Holly Berry House had so much *home* surrounding it.

They came to the cottage, and she stopped beneath the light on the porch. She looked down at her feet, and dug a little hole in the welcome mat with her shoe's pointy toe.

"Wyatt? Even though I didn't want the reward of our efforts once I got it, I have to thank you. You got me through some seriously rough emotional waters." She looked up at him. "I can't thank you enough. I have to somehow repay you. What can I do? Please, tell me."

An answer flew to mind, if not out of his mouth: actually go through with their relationship, as if it wasn't fake? But Wyatt couldn't ask for that. It was too much.

"You thought of something. I can see it in your eyes."

He had, but he wasn't going to say it. Not now. Maybe not ever. Sure, her dad gave permission, but Wyatt hadn't proved himself worthy yet. *It's not Mrs. Sutherland's approval for me joining the family I'm worried about now.*

It's my own. I need to show I'm worthy of Chelsea.

But how?

"Come in. I'll make us a hot cocoa while you make up your mind about how I can repay you." Chelsea unlocked the cottage door and Wyatt followed her into the cozy room. She made cocoa, and he lit a fire in the grate, while snippets of the conversation with Mom floated back to him.

Mom. I'm not giving up on Chelsea Sutherland. She's the best girl I know. She makes me want to be a better version of myself. To quit goofing off all the time. To be her match. He'd waxed poetic about Chelsea's perfections, and with every single one, Mom's face had grown icier until she'd become the quintessential Snow Queen right before Wyatt's eyes.

You nor I nor any of us will ever be enough for the Sutherlands. Just ask them.

It felt like a gut-kick even just recalling it. *I may not be worthy of them now, but I will prove to both you and to them that I am. I'm going to rock this challenge you and Dad foisted on me, and I'm going to prove that I've got business chops enough to give Chelsea a great life.*

Mom had smirked. *You just try it, son. But that's not what impresses Sutherlands. You have to be one of them. And you're not.*

But ... he was. Ike had given him one of those bear hugs that, if they were a mafia family instead of a school-principal and community-service type family, would have signified Wyatt was in and he'd have to die trying to get out.

What was her problem with the family? Mack! Mack had handed him a list of his research. It had fallen somewhere in Wyatt's car while Wyatt worried about ten dozen other things.

He'd find it, and he'd confront Mom.

Chelsea had put on some instrumental Christmas music, plugged in the lights on her tree, and dimmed the lights. She walked in with a mug, just as Wyatt got the fire coaxed into a good blaze and sat on the floor in front of the fire, waiting for Chelsea to join him.

"Now, what's your request?"

Should he or shouldn't he tell her?

"Chelsea, your dad and mom are great."

"I know, right?"

"Heath … is tolerable."

"Precisely. Especially at a distance. Some people are easier to love at a distance. Anyway, he'll probably mellow after the baby comes. I hear fatherhood softened my dad, too."

Really? Huh. "I bet that's true. Heath is going to be a good dad."

"You'll be a fun dad someday." Chelsea sipped her steaming cocoa with an audible slurp. "Really fun."

But not a dad Chelsea would take seriously. Was that her implication? Wyatt set his cup down. It was now or never.

"Chelsea, I did think of a way you can help me."

"Oh?"

"I've got an assignment at North Star Capital, and my parents are putting my feet to the fire with it. It's a test, more or less, and I'm not sure I'm up to it."

"I'm sure you'll do fine. And if you don't, They'll give you more chances. They're your parents." When Wyatt lifted a brow, she backed off a little. "Well. Anyway, they love you in their way. They do want to see you succeed."

Uh-huh. "I need them to believe I will succeed, whether I can or not. Their belief that I can handle the *mathematical* aspects of a job in finance is what matters right now."

Chelsea's face fell. "What are you asking of me, exactly?"

121

Chapter 19

Chelsea

No. It couldn't be. Wyatt couldn't *possibly* be asking her to crunch the numbers for the investment test his parents gave him—to pull the wool over Mr. and Mrs. North's eyes and make them think he was mathematically competent, when ... was he? Or wasn't he?

Her soul hollowed out, filling with echoes of past guys asking her to do their math assignments. Always—every time—it had been a prelude to their dumping her. Time after time, she'd given in, and with Fargo, she'd even bought into the charade.

And it had nearly sunk her. It had made her forget who she was for so long. Only Wyatt had rebuilt that. But, had it all just been a lead-up? For *this?*

"Wyatt, I—"

"It'd just be for this one investment list."

It's just for this one statistics class, babe. Fargo's words floated back to her. *It's not cheating if we do the work together. It's tutoring. I'm the one holding the pencil and the calculator.*

"I'd be the one making the final decision and recommendation." Wyatt sat on the rug at her feet in front of the fire he'd just built, but with every word he was dousing the fire that he'd kindled inside her heart. "You'd just be helping me determine the ROI. Return on investment."

"And you can't run the numbers yourself? Doesn't the firm have some kind of software for that?"

"I mean, I can. Er, I want to."

What did he mean, exactly? That he wanted Chelsea to do the work and then he would take the credit? It was *far* too reminiscent of Fargo's courses required to get into business school. "You'd be using my skills and then claiming the victory."

"Yeah." Wyatt's face fell. "I mean, no. I mean—here. I'll show it to you. Look. I have the spreadsheet right here, as well as some raw data."

Accepting it like her fingers were hot tongs to kill the bacteria of his phone screen's information, Chelsea scanned the cells of the spreadsheet. Real estate investments, a car dealership, an airplane manufacturer, at the bottom, separated a little from the rest, a startup for novelty items. Cheery Feet, how cheesy.

"What about playing to your audience? Just pick the one your parents are recommending." She handed back the phone. "Then if you win, great, and they feel good about it. If you lose money on the investment, it's not all on you."

Wyatt leaned back on the sheepskin rug and shut his eyes. "I thought of that. But I really want to do something for North Star Capital, but also something good for Sugarplum Falls."

"Are any of these investments centered here in town?" She set down her cocoa. It didn't taste good anymore. "The spreadsheet column with locations of businesses reads like a map of Caldwell City."

"Yeah. I know. But a couple do have ties here. Distant."

"I don't think I can help you with—" Her earlier earnest begging for him to tell her how she could help him echoed in her ears. It was stupid to promise she'd give him something and then rescind it. *I could do it, but at what cost?* "Did you just now think of asking me to help you with this project?"

"I mean, it's been brewing in my mind for a while."

"How long?"

"Ever since I got the list from them a couple of weeks ago. You're the numbers queen. I'm the people prince."

Royalty. Wow.

Chelsea closed her eyes and rubbed her temples. "So, since before you offered to be my fake boyfriend and then my fake fiancé."

"Um ..." Wyatt looked stricken.

A roaring began in her ears, louder than a blizzard's wind. "Was any of this real to you, Wyatt?" Blast her voice for cracking!

He'd said he was having a hard time distinguishing fiction from reality.

123

But the truth was, Chelsea had more or less given up the idea that it was fake the second Dad gave permission for them to marry and Heath hugged her.

"Chelsea, this has nothing to do with …" His voice trailed off, like he couldn't finish the lie.

"And the engagement?"

Wyatt's face hardened. "Was it real to you?"

Was his tone mocking, or sincere? In her haze she couldn't decipher it. And moreover, how could she answer that—and not open up her soul to more abuse?

"You told me your family's opinion took precedence." His temples pulsed.

"It does." Dad and Heath were fine with Wyatt. Mom? It wasn't clear. She'd been busy, what with the wedding, but she hadn't sounded thrilled, and then she did call Wyatt unreliable the other day. "But any holdouts in my family about us are not what we're talking about here, because what I'm gathering from this conversation is this whole thing—dating, courting, engagement—was just a way to get me to do your math homework. All of this. None out of sincerity. The shopping and the flirting and the kisses were … ?" Her nose started to sting.

Wyatt opened his eyes and sat up straight. "It's not like that, Chelsea."

Sure, it wasn't. *Fool me once, men, shame on me.* Her eyes got blurry.

"Look, I know in my enthusiasm, I said I'd do anything to repay you, but … that's just—I don't know how you could ask me *that* when—" Her voice hitched and she had to sniffle.

"When what?"

Her tears turned from salty to sour. "I'm glad we could be of use to each other." She pulled off his grandma's ring and shoved it into his palm. "It was a beautiful diamond. Thank you for letting me pretend. For a minute."

He stared down at it. "Chelsea!"

"See yourself out." She went to her bedroom and closed the door, falling on her bed. She pushed her face into her pillow to muffle any errant sobs.

Again. Used again. I'm nothing but a calculator with breasts. And maybe not even very impressive breasts.

124

An hour later, she went out to shut off the lights. In the living room, she bumped the coffee table with her leg, and the tiles of the Scrabble game scattered. She half-closed the board, making a V, and poured all their arranged words into the velvet bag.

I'm done keeping score with him. It's over.

Back in her bedroom, she tore off her pretty new dress and tossed it onto the floor of the closet, where—ah. Good. One last pair of gray sweatpants lay, having escaped the trash truck. She stepped into them, yanked an old boyfriend sweater from the bottom of the laundry basket, washed off her makeup, and climbed into her bed.

She pulled the blanket over her head.

Chapter 20

Wyatt

After an aimless, all-night drive around Sugarplum Falls, a bedraggled Wyatt pulled into the parking lot at North Star Capital, got out and leaned against his car.

I can't go in there. And not just because he hadn't showered or brushed his teeth since yesterday.

"Hey, man." Up walked Mack, carrying a white paper sack with the Sugarbabies Bakery logo. "You look awful. No one saw you after you and Chelsea left that party last night, so I thought *awesome for Wyatt.* But looking at you now, I'm thinking *not awesome.*"

Definitely not awesome. "What's in the sack?" He reached out, as if to beg for something to take away the bad taste in his mouth he'd put there by his own stupidity.

"Gingerbread men."

He dropped his hand. Of course. Ginger.

Mack inched away. "I'd better get in there. Mrs. North wanted to see me. I suspect it's another list she wants me to pass you."

"Of investments?"

"More likely a list of the *women Wyatt should be dating instead of Chelsea Sutherland.* Since you're officially engaged, I would have thought she'd given up. Any normal woman would. Of course, it's Drusilla North we're talking about here. Bulldozers with cut brake lines give up sooner." Mack shoved his hands deeper into his coat pockets when he didn't get so much as a courtesy laugh. "Hey, did I tell you? I was a fly on the wall for a discussion between your parents. There's one particular investment on that list they sent—and they're banking on the fact you'll choose it."

Well, wouldn't that make everything he'd stirred up last night go away?

126

Maybe Wyatt should just hear it out. "Which one?"

"A startup of some kind. A real opportunity for North Star, they said."

"Mom mentioned that." But because it was a late-comer and Wyatt had been occupied, he hadn't looked into it much yet. "I'll check it more thoroughly."

"Not that I know all the particulars, but I know your parents, and I know they're pulling for you to choose it. Check your email, they've sent more prospectus materials for it than any other item on your list."

From what scant info Wyatt recalled about the numbers, that startup was by far the least appealing investment opportunity they'd sent. "It's not centered in Sugarplum Falls."

"Like I said, look deeper into ownership. There could be ties you're looking for, so don't write it off completely just because of the first glance. You do want to make Mom and Dad happy, right?"

Since he couldn't make anyone else on planet earth happy, he might as well give it a harder look. "Fine."

Up drove a sports car. Mom emerged from it, stalking across the employee lot, eyes laser-trained on Wyatt. "You received my list from Mack, I take it? That's why you're loitering out here? To discuss it in private?"

Mack jumped. "No, Mrs. North, I was just heading upstairs to print it out for him. I know you wanted him to have a hard copy."

"Don't disappoint me, Mack." Mom whirled on Wyatt as soon as Mack was out of earshot. Her breath didn't steam like everyone else's. *Probably because it came from her ice-cold soul.* "I thought about it all night, what you said to me."

"And?" Wyatt was too tired to argue anymore.

"And there will be no Sutherland joining the North family."

What was she, a prophetess? "Mom, you have got to tell me what you have against that family."

Mom exhaled loudly. "I thank you for at least not following her name with a sappy *the woman I love.*" She rolled her eyes. "I'm going to want that ring back. And now."

Fine. He reached in his pocket, dug it out and shoved it into Mom's hand.

She looked down at her palm, and then back up at Wyatt—not as triumphantly as he would have expected.

He huffed out a sigh. "You happy now? I'm pretty tired." Far too tired to be having this conversation, which was more like a haranguing. "Answer me something. What is your problem with Chelsea? I need to know specifics. And don't just tell me she's a Sutherland. Anything any previous Sutherland has done to you in the deep past can't be relevant."

He'd reread the list from Mack late last night, trying to make headway into Mom's mindset, but it all seemed so petty.

"Oh, I have nothing against Chelsea personally. Not at all. She's all right as a separate entity."

"So it's her Sutherland connections, then." Which would explain her disdain for Heath, too, as well as all her anti-Sutherland comments. "Ike wasn't the principal when you went to high school, so I can't imagine you're a holding a grudge toward him."

"Not against Ike, no."

Ugh. This was the worst game of twenty questions of all time. "Quit making me guess here, or I'll start guessing myself."

"You'd never guess."

Oh, wouldn't he? "A Sutherland won the town spelling bee when you were a child, leaving you as the runner-up."

Mom stiffened. "How do you know that?"

"A Sutherland tried out for junior varsity volleyball the same time as you. She made the team, and you did not."

"She couldn't even spike. You should have seen her serve. Her uncle was the coach."

Wyatt scanned the note from Mack mentally. "A Sutherland auditioned to sing the National Anthem at the ballpark the year that the high school baseball team won the state championship, and she was chosen instead of you."

"I was pitch-perfect. Not a screech in sight. Her mother was the vocal instructor, and I was nobody."

Hardly nobody. Her daddy had owned the one bank in town. "The Miss Sugarplum Falls pageant? I've never heard of it."

"It was a big deal back in the day, believe me. I deserved the crown, and—"

"Don't tell me. A Sutherland got it."

"Not technically, but someone who later married into the Sutherland family. Are you seeing a pattern here yet, son? Every single move I made—from birth until I was able to get myself out of this town for college—a Sutherland blocked me. This is a place where I can't win. Ever. Because I don't have the right last name. They are in every aspect of this town's existence. It's infested with Sutherlands."

"You're saying the family pulls strings? Exercises nepotism? Favors their own?" Those were pretty big accusations. "Tell me, Mom. How was your volleyball serve?"

"Not ... stellar. It usually hit the net, but I was taller by four inches. I could block the other team's serve."

Uh-huh. "There has to be more to it, Mom."

"There's not." But the way she said it, Wyatt inferred there was. Something deeper, maybe even darker. She was really hung up on something. "Now, I'll thank you to stop prying into my past to try to make excuses for your girlfriend. She's having no part of North Star Bank. I mean, Capital. No Sutherland is getting her fingers in my daddy's company. One Sutherland touches it, and they all think it belongs to them. They're contagious." Mom looked almost crazed. "They're this town, and it's them, and I'm sick of all of them."

"Mom, I think you're not seeing things clearly." What could be the big thing blocking her view of reality. Mom wasn't like this in other areas of her life. There had to be more.

Dad walked up. "Is she giving you a rough time, son?" He was holding a drink-holder tray and handed Mom a thermal cup from The Cider Press.

"Don't you go unveiling my past, Deacon." She took the cup from him, despite her obvious hostility. "I've got a right to my secrets."

"Not when your past spills into present-day hostility and affects our relationship with our son—and his with a woman he obviously cares for deeply."

129

"That's not fair." Mom stomped her foot, and a puff of snow came up around it. "Do not tell him, Deacon, or so help me—"

"You'll tell him or I will." Wow. Dad was more adamant with Mom than Wyatt had ever seen him be.

Mom's shoulders sagged. "It's water under the bridge."

"If so, then why the grudge, Mom?" There was only so much of Mom and Dad he could take, especially on days like these, and there had been quite a few of them. Maybe Wyatt didn't want North Star Capital as his future.

Dad turned to Wyatt. "Son, meet me for lunch—*after* you've had a chance to clean yourself up and get some shut-eye. What? Don't you think I know how you look after you've pulled an all-nighter driving around town? Kindly recall that I've been your dad since you were a wayward teen."

Fine.

Wyatt went home, skipping whatever argument Mom foisted on Dad next to get him to change his mind about divulging her past to Wyatt.

However, even the promise of answers from Dad about Mom's Sutherland hang-ups wasn't enough to soothe his nerves about what had happened with Chelsea last night.

I wrecked it. She thinks this whole thing is me using her—from the beginning, like I set it up that way.

Speaking of hang-ups! There had to be backstory in Chelsea's reaction last night, more than just feeling used for her math skills.

He had to figure that out, and fast.

But who could tell him?

Oh, right. The one person likely to know, and one of the last people Wyatt wanted to ask. *What if she really doesn't want me in her family?*

***

"We so appreciated your song last night at the party, Wyatt." Mrs. Sutherland smiled and handed Wyatt his favorite sandwich, turkey with cranberry sauce and provolone on sourdough, grilled in the panini-maker. How did she have time to make this, with all the other things going on at her house? She was pretty amazing. *Just like her daughter.*

Speaking of amazing, the sandwich probably tasted amazing, but Wyatt

130

couldn't lift it to take a bite. Not while knowing that Mrs. Sutherland might show love but didn't feel much respect for him, at least not enough respect to accept him as a potential part of her daughter's life. She was the holdout on accepting him that Chelsea had mentioned.

Even Chelsea knows her mom has misgivings about me.

"It was good to sing together, the three of us, after a while without Heath coming to sing." Would she take his hint that he, Wyatt, had been the dependable one lately?

"Uh-huh." She sipped a cup of something hot and steaming. "Seems like with what's been going on between you and Chelsea, the group dynamics will have to change."

So she was worried about the singing group's future? *No, dimwit. She's worried about her daughter.* "Maybe so. Not necessarily." Especially if things worked out with him and Chelsea. *Or, if Chelsea kicks me to the curb and Christmas Tree-O is no more.*

Mrs. Sutherland sat beside him at the kitchen counter, picking at the crust of her sandwich. "Of necessity, though. I always knew the minute Heath found Odessa that Christmas Tree-O's days were numbered."

"Oh?" Wyatt set down his sandwich, still untasted. "Because you didn't think Chelsea and I could keep it afloat without Heath?"

"No, no. Not that at all." Mrs. Sutherland pushed her plate a little. "I mean, we all know Heath—that he'd still want to be in charge, but that he wouldn't put in the time because he, you know, moved, got married, is having a baby. He's gone, choosing other priorities. The right ones, but still. It can't be a trio."

Wyatt didn't come here expecting to feel like he was being sung a funeral dirge. "Sad."

"Not really. Just different. A duo is often even better than a trio."

Duo. "What? What duo?"

Mrs. Sutherland smiled on him, and it was like the glow from a just-lit Christmas tree after being in a dark room. "You and Chelsea, of course. I heard the two of you sing together all season. Your blend is so much better without Heath."

Um. "You think?" Why was he letting himself get distracted by music talk, when there were so many other important questions right now? And why let himself feel this good when she wasn't approving *Chelsea and Wyatt*, just the singing duo?

"I don't just think, I know. I might be a culinary teacher these days, but I have a degree in music. Vocal performance."

She did? No wonder her house was filled with music. "I never knew that."

"That's okay. What you do need to know is that you and Chelsea make a very good duo." She met his eyes meaningfully. "Not just singing."

"But I thought … Excuse me, Mrs. Sutherland, but I was getting a different vibe from you the other day."

Iris Sutherland inhaled deeply, exhaled and looked at Wyatt pointedly. "I didn't mean to let you see that."

"What is it? I know I'll never be good enough for your daughter. She's—" There weren't adjectives strong enough for how great Chelsea was. "She's above me in every way."

Mrs. Sutherland shook her head. "Wyatt, how could you think that? You're like a bonus son to me. The third kid we could never have."

Well, that was what Wyatt had always felt from Mrs. Sutherland, until lately. "I don't understand. When Chelsea and I turned up dating, I definitely got a chill." One he was used to getting from Mom. Easy to recognize, due to plenty of practice.

"No, no, no." She went to the fridge and pulled out a soda bottle for each of them, placing one in front of Wyatt. His favorite kind, too. "My misgivings—which were not classy to let show—had nothing to do with you."

"Then what?" He shouldn't press her, but this was important. "I need to know."

Mrs. Sutherland closed her eyes for a minute. "It's not about you." Clearly, the topic pained her. "I know logically that your mother won't mistreat Chelsea if the two of you marry, but …"

Wyatt held up a hand to stop her. *Mom. Again!* "Was that what bothered you? My mom's"—there was no way to put it other than bluntly—"bad personality?"

A little snort of humor escaped Mrs. Sutherland's nose. "That's one way to put it. And I wish I hadn't let the thought enter my mind. She will be kind to Chelsea, right?"

That was something Wyatt couldn't guarantee. *I need to work to change her mind—about whatever it is.* Step one was go to that meeting with Dad and find out what Mom's problem with Sutherlands was.

"Wyatt, honey." Mrs. Sutherland took a bite of her sandwich and then washed it down with soda. "Chelsea's been happier in the past few weeks than I've seen her in ages. I'm not blind. I know it's thanks to you."

To him? But yes, Chelsea had seemed happier. "I really do care for her."

"She's finally acting like someone cares for her—including caring for herself." Mrs. Sutherland's eyes crinkled at the sides. "Like I said, I do love that duo."

Could she really mean it? Wyatt's gut leaped, but then it crashed down. There wasn't going to be any duo. Not after what Wyatt had done last night to infuriate Chelsea and destroy her trust. "Can you tell me something, Mrs. Sutherland? I want to ask Chelsea, but she's upset with me."

"Oh?"

"She thinks I've been using her." Saying it aloud made it feel a hundred times worse. "I can't understand what I did wrong, but her whole demeanor changed when I asked her for help with some numbers I needed to evaluate for work."

"Numbers." Mrs. Sutherland's brow furrowed and she set down her food. "You must not know, then." She beckoned for him to follow her out onto the new-fallen snow in the grassy area behind Holly Berry House. "Wyatt, I would gladly tell you the story of a young girl who'd never been anybody's girlfriend before, and the opportunistic young man who took advantage of that fact. However, you and I both know it's going to be best if you hear it from Chelsea."

True, but there was a big barrier to that. "Actually, she's not speaking to me."

"That could make it tough." They looked out over the snow toward Holly

Berry Cottage. "I'll try to think of something, but this is between you and Chelsea. I don't believe in interfering."

Unlike some mothers!

"Well, if you can think of anything I can do to fix it, I will do it. I'll do anything to convince her I'm sincere."

Anything. *I'm that in love with her.*

Chapter 21

Chelsea

Chelsea slaved away over her big pharmaceutical statistics until her head hurt. Or, more like even though her head already hurt.

Numbers. Numbers. Numbers. They crunched when she added, subtracted, and calculated. Much like her feelings every time she thought about being asked to evaluate numbers for men who she mistakenly believed cared for her—for the essence of Chelsea, not just for the mathematician part of her.

For now, though, she wasn't touching Wyatt or his project. It might be a while before she could.

Some of her hair had fallen out of the messy bun before Mom had come to visit with the bowl of Christmas stew yesterday morning. It still sat in the soup mug on the counter, cold, and untouched. Mom had said. *"Eat. And forgive."*

Well, forgiveness was up for debate, but in the meantime, how could Chelsea eat? Fools didn't deserve to eat. Or get dressed in anything but baggy, unlaundered clothes.

The second she hit submit on her work project, she crawled back into bed.

Not a moment later, a knock sounded on the door of Holly Berry Cottage. Chelsea groaned and poked her head out from under the blankets. "Go away. I'm not taking visitors."

Mom had already been by and dropped off a gingerbread cake on the porch. A pretty one, with a snowdrift of white icing and decorated with little sage leaves and tiny red berries. But all Chelsea could think was *Good. It's got ginger so I won't have to share a single bite with Wyatt.*

Peevish much?

"Chelsea? Are you in there?" A silhouette darkened her bedroom window, with a man's face coming near.

Oh, no! "Who's there?" Chelsea grabbed at the bedding. Not that she had anything to hide. Her gray sweats were as modest as modest could be. "Intruders will be prosecuted."

"Chelsea?" the man said again.

Man. Wait, was it Wyatt? Oh, he'd better not come bothering her, pressuring her to help him.

"It's me. Your cousin Mack. I need to talk to you."

Mack? Really? What the heck was he doing here? "One second." She hustled to the bathroom and did a one-minute repair job on her appearance, even though she could have used several hours' repair after the hibernation she'd done. "I'm coming."

She opened the door and let in a frigid wind. Mack looked half frost-bitten. "Brr. That weather is no joke."

"Winters in Sugarplum Falls never are."

He bustled in, patting his sides. "Anywhere cold enough to freeze a waterfall solid isn't joking around in temperature."

"Sorry for the delay." Ooh, she shouldn't have left him out in it so long. "Come sit by the fireplace." There was no fire in it, of course. "Can I make you something hot to drink?"

Mack refused a drink and sat down in one of the wingback chairs. He fidgeted like he was sitting on a pinecone. "I'm just going to be blunt, since I don't really have any lead-ups. I know you're mad at Wyatt."

Was she ever. "Don't tell me you're here to drop off his financial conundrum for me to evaluate." Coward sent a proxy? "Because I've thought about it and no. I'm not doing it."

Mack bent forward and put his head in his hands, not his usual stance.

What was up with Mack? Hmm.

"I came to plead for Wyatt. Please don't put this situation on him when *I'm* the one who told him to ask you for help. Believe me—he said no. A lot of times. He said getting you to do his work would be like using you."

He'd said that? All the frigid wind went out of Chelsea's lungs. "It would," she said flatly.

"What happened was, when he got truly desperate, I pushed him. I told him that a girlfriend who was in love with him would want to help him no

136

matter what."

"Normally, that would be true." But she wasn't sure how she felt about Wyatt after the other night. Numb. Lost.

"He told me how you reacted, Chelsea, so I went to your mom, and she told me to come to you—but not until after she gave me a brief sketch of what had happened to you before."

Mom. Traitor. "What did she tell you, exactly?" Even Mom didn't know everything that had happened with Fargo.

"That guys had wanted to use you for your brain. Particularly your math skills. Guys that were unkind."

Unkind was putting it kindly. Chelsea pushed her toes deeper into her puppy-face socks and tried not to hiccup. "Did you rush over and tell Wyatt all about me and my history of dating men who can't do math?"

"I came straight here to apologize to you. Not on Wyatt's behalf, but my own. For not knowing, and for butting in." Mack sighed heavily. "But don't forget, there's a lot more to Wyatt North than whether or not he can do math. I have a lot of respect for that guy. He's the only one in all of North Star Capital who stands up to Drusilla North. And that's been one of the best results of him dating you."

"What do you mean?"

"Just that he started digging in his heels against everything his mom suggested that he didn't agree with, but not until you two started dating."

Huh. Really? Chelsea had definitely seen Wyatt showing more willingness to push back against her lately. Like in the hallway at the Hot Cocoa Festival, for instance. And when he'd given Chelsea his grandma's ring. *Which I threw back in his face.*

"Honestly, Chelsea, he didn't know about whatever wounded you. He would *never* use you. Wyatt North genuinely cares about you and is a better man when he's with you. Give him another chance."

How could she hold Mack accountable for not knowing her deep wound? *Or Wyatt?*

The words came out like a squeak. "Tell him to send me the numbers."

Mack lit up. "So you'll forgive him?"

Probably. Maybe. It felt a little soon to decide that much. "I'll at least help him out of his dilemma."

Mack had a spring in his step as he left. But Chelsea wasn't quite ready to spring back all the way. Even if he hadn't wounded Chelsea intentionally, the wound was still there. *But I can at least make good on my promise to pay him back.*

At her computer a few minutes later, an email from Wyatt practically blinked like the star atop the tree in downtown Sugarplum Falls.

With a terrible mix of feelings, she clicked on it.

It was the list of investment opportunities for Wyatt to choose from, accompanied as promised by raw data from Wyatt's additional research, according to the notes in the sidebars.

After a while evaluating and inputting them into a formula she created, Chelsea made an initial evaluation. Clearly, several of these weren't good risks based on multiple risk factors beyond investor control. The raw data Wyatt had collected was actually pretty telling. From this, he should probably be able to make his own decision. *Why does he need me to do this?*

Except ... yeah. While it was easy for her, that didn't mean it was easy for him. Just like talking to people who wanted to grill her about relationships wasn't easy for Chelsea.

Still, now that she'd lined them all out, the batches of numbers were very telling. Even Wyatt would be able to see the rankings plain as day.

Real estate was a strong possibility, the hospital absolutely not. The airplane manufacturing business looked promising, but he'd be crazy to put his money into a cruise line. Cruise line! Please. The ocean was hours away. Didn't he want to use the capital to infuse more life in the Sugarplum Falls economy? Give someone in this town a big Christmas surprise? Improve the local quality of life?

If that were the case, and he'd said as much, two stood out. First was the startup that seemed to have ties to Sugarplum Falls, Cheery Feet. It had a post office box listed in this town, although not its operational headquarters.

As a startup, maybe it didn't have an office space yet.

Not bad data. Not the best numerical data. But it did meet the Sugarplum

Falls connection criteria. It climbed to the top of her recommendation list.

She sat back in her chair and pulled at her tangle of hair, still writhing with feelings, despite Mack's reassurances. Half of her ached to believe him. Half of her was a realist. A realist based on personal life-experience.

No matter what Mack claimed, there was still a very real possibility that Wyatt had only dated her to mess with her mind and get what he wanted from her. That he'd been planning to dump her as soon as he turned in his report to his parents. All Chelsea had done was preempt his dumping.

But that hurt, too. Being the dumper was at least as gut-wrenching as being the dumpee, it turned out. *That's because my feelings are real. He's not only someone I fell in love with, he's been my best friend. My only long-time relationship, other than with family.*

Now that she'd cast him off like a used rag, who was the user? Chelsea. Wyatt could get a replacement for her in a snap. There was no incentive for him to take her back now that she'd proved so fickle. So, whether or not she was sorry for her rash move, chances were strong it was over between Wyatt and her.

Once she finalized what she'd promised, he would walk away.

Then she could get back under the covers of her bed and forget Wyatt North ever existed, just as surely as he would forget about Chelsea.

One last look at the data she'd evaluated, and she was ready to give Wyatt her recommendation, Cheery Feet. Just to dot her *I*'s and cross her *T*'s, she did a cursory final search to confirm Wyatt's findings.

Cheery Feet, novelty socks manufacturer and distributor for the entire Caldwell City region. President and CEO—no! Not him. It couldn't be.

But it most certainly was.

The Cheery Feet startup belonged to Fargo Frye. *Can I tell him to invest here?*

Chapter 22

Wyatt

C hristmas music filled the restaurant. Wyatt shifted in his chair and bumped his water glass, splashing it over the rim when his lunch buddy arrived.

"Son?"

Whoa. Dad hadn't come to talk to Wyatt after all. It was Mom herself.

"I see you ordered Dad's favorite already." She frowned like her life depended on it.

"Yeah. Chicken Caesar." Even if the croutons on the salad were fresh baked and delicious, Mom's tale was not going to be, judging from her stiff demeanor. Wyatt broke the ice. "Why'd you decide to come instead of Dad?"

"Because he doesn't know all the details. He couldn't." Mom looked at her nails, which she always did when she was squirming on the inside. She was a great financial negotiator when she had the upper hand, but if not, she had that terrible tell. "I never told him everything." She looked up.

It was a long story, but the upshot was this: in spite of her spite against all Sutherlands for their thwarting her ambitions, all through high school, Mom had dated a Sutherland son. Not Ike Sutherland—for the obvious reason that he'd been already smitten with Iris, Chelsea's mom, from the time he was a kid.

No, Mom had fallen head over heels for Ike's older brother Zeke.

"Really? Zeke." Zeke, Zeke, the Black Sheep. Chelsea's family called him that—at his own insistence.

"Zeke Sutherland." Mom stabbed at her romaine a few times but didn't eat any. "But he didn't want me as much as he wanted other things."

"As in?"

"As in"—she chucked her fork into her bowl with a clatter—"that

Sutherland family! They have this *obsession* with Sugarplum Falls. Its prosperity. Its future. Its image. You know what? It's *maddening*."

Uh, okay? "You're saying Zeke chose the town? Over his relationship with you?" That would sting, but it hardly seemed likely. Zeke rarely even showed up in Sugarplum Falls.

Mom stirred her salad but didn't eat. "He told me his family expected him to make Sugarplum Falls a top priority."

"Above everything else? Even his own relationships?" Wyatt was missing something. "But you didn't want to choose the town, I take it."

"Of course not!" Mom slammed her fork down. "I wanted more. I wanted to do something with the gifts I was given. I wanted to get somewhere far away from the rest of the Sutherlands."

"But you stayed."

"Yes. And I did do something big with those gifts."

This was not the moment for this question, but it slipped out. "As in taking the North Star Bank you inherited from your parents and turning it into North Star Capital. An investment firm instead of a local bank."

"Exactly. I made it something bigger, better. You watch—we'll be moving on from this small place."

"I thought you liked it here." Who wouldn't? Sugarplum Falls was the kind of town everybody's secret heart wished they lived in. Nice neighbors, clean streets, friendly faces, the Christmas Spirit year-round. *And it has Chelsea.*

"Then you don't know me at all," Mom said darkly.

Maybe not. What child really did know a parent, though? Ever? The very hierarchical structure of the relationship prevented it. "Then why build North Forty?" Why put down architectural roots? *She does keep it cold in there.*

"So that we can prove to our clients that we are prosperous, so they will come to us as business partners and believe their project will succeed. Even out-of-towners can be impressed by North Forty."

It was all about appearances. Of course it was. "Back to Zeke. So, he chose the town."

"That Sutherland family will always choose the town over what will

141

benefit them most. And they choose each other over anyone outside their little clique."

Clique? More like family. That wasn't the same thing. And the Sutherlands were notoriously inclusive! Mom had this all wrong.

"So, are you saying that *you* would have been the best thing for Zeke Sutherland?"

"Of course. I could have taken him places. I had my inheritance. He wouldn't have had to spend decades wandering, trying to find himself."

Uh, that was not likely accurate. Chances were, Zeke would still have wandered—and bled Mom dry in the process, financially and more. Surely, she would have grown tired of that and frustrated with him and … crunch. Implosion of that relationship.

"And do you really think that Zeke would have been best for *you,* rather than Dad?" Dad and Mom were so much on the same page—except, possibly, that Dad loved Sugarplum Falls and was happier to stay here than Mom was. But he didn't mind trying to level up the bank to an investment firm. "Not Dad?" he asked again, softer this time.

Mom stilled. She met his gaze, blinking a long time. "Of—of course not. I love your father. He's my other half."

It was as if this line of thinking passed through her brain for the first time, and she needed to process the idea from every angle before reacting.

The rejection by Zeke had obviously been the final nail in the coffin of her patience with the family. But she was still standing by with the hammer ready to pound more nails.

So unnecessary. And from the look softening on Mom's face, it was becoming clear to her as well.

"I know something that might offer you some measure of vindication." Wyatt pushed his salad plate back. If there was one thing Mom loved it was vindication. "Let me tell you what I know about Zeke."

"Go on, then." She picked up her water glass with a slosh.

"What I know is that Chelsea's uncle Zeke insists that everyone in the Sutherland family call him the black sheep of the family. He's been through a dozen careers, just while *I've* known them. Just got a new one, from what I hear."

Mom set down her water glass and tilted her head to the side. "He didn't stick around. I knew that. But he didn't stick around *anywhere ever?* That's not very Sutherland of him."

"Yep, he finished divinity school and is conducting the mayor's daughter's wedding this weekend." Tonight, actually. At Holly Berry House. *And I'm not going to be there. At least not at Chelsea's side as her fiancé.* "Mom, you would never have liked to be with someone who didn't like to settle down to one career path in life. It wouldn't have been a slow path to insanity, it would have been a bullet train."

"I mean, if he'd chosen me, I could have made him do it."

Um, probably not. "What else I know? He's had five wives. None of them could get him to stay with a career. Now, granted, you're probably more strong-minded than any of them could have been"—than any other woman Wyatt had ever met—"but that would have been a daily battle. I'm so glad you chose Dad. Can you imagine North Star with someone like Zeke at your side instead?"

For a second, she shuddered. Then, she iced up again. Her chin bunched. "No one ever broke up with me, Wyatt. No one. I was the one who did the breaking up."

Ah, that made sense! Finally!

Rejection. She'd faced it and never healed. Not even by allowing Dad's devotion to work its way into her soul to patch it up.

Wyatt stared at the salt and pepper shakers between them and spoke in his quietest voice. "Let it go, Mom. Let *his memory* go. He was never the guy for you."

He looked up at her, and Mom's face morphed, almost breaking. Was she going to cry? Mom never, ever cried. But her chin was trembling.

Her voice cracked. "It was always what the Sutherlands wanted, what the town needed. He chose that. He chose them. Their opinions. Their preferences."

Wyatt stiffened. Mom's assertions rang like an iron pipe on corrugated steel. But he had to push on. This was about Mom right now.

143

"No, actually. He didn't choose that—or them." Uncle Zeke might have talked the Sutherland family's doctrine, but he hadn't lived it. Not one bit. "If instead, he had chosen them and their values, I think he would have been happier." Or at least steadier. Zeke the Black Sheep might be very happy, for all Wyatt knew. There was more than one way to live happily. Although, a trail of broken marriages hinted at unhappiness, for certain.

Mom huffed a long sigh. "I never saw him again. I thought it was because I was purposely avoiding every Sutherland in Sugarplum Falls."

"More like he left on his walkabout and never came back. I spend a lot of time with the Sutherlands, and I only hear tales of him. If I go to the wedding this weekend"—which he wouldn't, since Chelsea wouldn't want him there— "I'll set eyes on him for the first time." He whipped out his phone and did an internet search on the name Zeke Sutherland and Sugarplum Falls. Up popped a few photos.

Ooh, very scraggly. Definitely not the guy you'd hire to be your department store Santa, despite the long white beard. "This, Mom? *This* is the guy you have hated Sutherlands for all these years? The guy you spent more than five seconds wishing he hadn't broken up with you?"

He held it out for her, and when Mom lay eyes on it, she recoiled, mouthing *ew*. "He has really let himself go. But those are definitely his eyes." She winced. "What's happened to his countenance? He looks really hardened."

It was an older picture. "Maybe it's just a bad photo." Or maybe he'd hit rock bottom and grasped at hope by choosing his latest career.

"Wow. I guess I didn't really know him. Or any of them. I can't believe I wasted time feeling sorry that he dumped me, when all along I should have been doing a jig of joy at my escape."

"We have to stop letting the past color our perceptions. Please don't judge Heath or Chelsea by Zeke—the Zeke jerk-to-you back then or the roughed up version of him now. Chelsea is"—he gulped to keep the quaver out of his voice—"practically perfect. And I need her in my life, Mom."

Mom bit her lips together, and her eyes were glossy.

"But that's not all." Wyatt stood, went around the table, and knelt. "Mom, I need *you* in my life." He put his arm around her shoulders. They were

144

quaking. "Not just the businesswoman you. The *mom* you."

The quaking increased, but no tears fell. "You're right. I know what you're implying, that I haven't been the nurturing mom."

"You've been the mom I needed, though. Imagine how wild I would have run without your firm guidance, eh?" He cracked a smile. "Come on!"

Mom glanced at the ceiling and then back at Wyatt. "Let's not even go there. Your antics wouldn't have ended in the principal's office, they would have ended with the police." She heaved a heavy sigh. "That principal was a good help to you. I know you acted up in school just for the chance to go hang out with him, pick his brain on random topics."

She knew that? Wyatt searched his soul. Yeah, that was actually correct.

"Don't look so shocked that I know that. He knew it, too. We discussed it a few times. Ike Sutherland was just the right balance between sternness and amusement at what all you pulled during high school. I really do owe him a debt of gratitude for not being too heavy-handed with the punishments. Other administrators might not have been so merciful."

Exactly! "If you really feel that way, then embrace *his* children in your life." Like Ike had embraced her child. "There's no better way to win someone's respect than to be kind to their kids. Let Chelsea in, Mom. She's really someone worth loving."

"Are you sincerely saying you love her, Wyatt? I wasn't sure if you meant it the other night."

"I am. I do." He did. He loved her. So much. "I have loved her for a long time, but it's never been a good time to act on it."

"And now is?"

"Even Heath gives me the thumbs up." As had Ike, and all the aunts. Even Chelsea's mom—especially if he could accomplish this, right here, of getting Mom to thaw toward the Sutherland family, and to Chelsea in particular. "I love her. But I love you, too."

"You're a good son." Mom actually hugged him back. "I will think about what you said. And"—the next words seemed to take great effort—"make no mistake. No matter what old wounds you saw laid raw in me today, I'm glad every single day that I married your dad so we could build a life together *and* have a wise son like you. Chelsea is a lucky girl."

"If she chooses me, I'm the lucky one." He hugged Mom, and she dug in to her salad.

Wyatt returned to his chair, staring at his food. Unfortunately, Chelsea was the one hold-out about giving the thumbs up.

His phone pinged. *Email from Chelsea Sutherland.* "I have to go read this."

But when he did, his eyes nearly fell out of their sockets. *How can she be suggesting this to me?*

He had to go see her. Right now.

"Before you go, son"—Mom rooted around in her purse—"here. You should have this back." She handed him Grandma's ring. "If you love her, don't let her get away."

Chapter 23

Chelsea

Again with the door-knocking. If it was someone trying to drag her out the door and over to the Fargo Frye/Esther Lang wedding happening at Mom and Dad's house, they could just forget it.

She burrowed deeper into her covers.

"Chelsea?" A man's muffled voice came through the door.

"Go away, Mack. I did what you asked me to do, now leave me alone." *I'm not going to that wedding no matter what.*

This time, however, it wasn't Mack. It was the last person she wanted to see in this state of dishevelment. "Chelsea?"

Oh, no. Not Wyatt!

"No, you can't come in." She huddled under the covers, still in the same sweats and nasty sweater from three nights ago. Her hair she'd washed in the sink, but her working-from-home uniform needed laundering something fierce. "I'm not taking visitors."

"Chelsea. I got your email. I need several answers."

"I'm not taking questions, either." Not taking questions! As if she was a politician being chased by a reporter. "Just read what I said in the email and go with it." Half of her wanted to go to him, to see whether he was just here to say thanks and dump her, but the other half ached to know if what Mack said was true. The dual-mindedness paralyzed her.

"Chelsea. It's freezing out here. And my car ran out of gas on the way up the driveway to Holly Berry House. I had to walk from a half-mile away."

"Why were you out of gas?"

"I spent a full night driving around, thinking after you kicked me out. I haven't thought to buy fuel since then. I haven't thought of much else but you."

Oh, her heart! The temperature out there had to be below zero. Add the wind that blew specially out of the canyon onto the hill of Holly Berry House, and she couldn't exactly let him catch pneumonia.

"Fine. But give me five minutes." Mack got one minute, but for Wyatt she'd need five. He was younger and could stave off frostbite longer anyway.

She whipped off the misshapen sweater and shoved it onto the floor of the closet, kicking it to the back. The nearest blouse was emerald green, and she tugged it on. Instant transformation, thanks to Amélie and Gregor. Wow. And thanks to Wyatt for buying it for her. *I feel pretty in everything he gave me.*

"Chelsea?" Wyatt's voice rang through the house. "Sorry, but your door was open, and I have manicotti that is getting cold."

"Manicotti?" Her mind emptied of every other thought. She hadn't eaten anything but eggnog and hot cocoa for a couple of days. She ventured out of her room toward the kitchen area of the cottage.

"I thought you threw those things away." His eyes were on her legs. "Never mind. You're beautiful even in the Gray Sweats of Shame."

Nice. "Stop talking about my wardrobe and hand over the Mario's." She grabbed plates and forks from the kitchen. "When I said I wasn't taking questions, I meant it. Especially no questions until after we've eaten." And probably none then, either.

They said grace, and then she downed her manicotti in a matter of about ninety seconds, the ricotta and mozzarella and oregano blending in a perfect filling for the tubular pasta. Oh, and that incredible marinara sauce, with its fresh tomato flavor, and just the right hint of basil and garlic. "Mmm. This is amazing. And it's even more amazing because I was starving."

"You hadn't eaten?" Wyatt looked alarmed. "Since when?"

"I told you I'm not taking questions."

"I want to ask three."

"Zero."

"Make it five then."

"Fine, three. But I don't promise to answer. Just to take the question." She dragged her breadstick through the final remnant of the marinara.

148

"You're being stubborn." Wyatt picked up their plates and took them to the sink where he began to wash them. "But I deserve it. Sorry. I mean, I know I deserve it, although I think I'm missing the deeper reasons why. All I can think is there has to be more to why you got so upset."

Lots more.

"So, you can probably guess my first question."

Uh, yeah. She could. And it had to do with her wild reaction to his plea for help, based on her personal history with Fargo's cruelty. *I couldn't stop myself.* "Mack didn't come talk to you? He came to see me, you know."

"He did?" Wyatt looked shocked. He wasn't one to feign surprise. "Whoa, whoa, whoa. When did that happen?"

So maybe Wyatt really didn't know anything about her past. "Next question. Skip that one. I'm sure the second one is the most important anyway. I can already guess what it is, as well."

"Oh, yeah?"

Yeah, she could. It was almost guaranteed to be a follow-up question to the email recommendation. She'd give him that answer, he'd take or leave her advice, and then he'd be gone from her life. Just like Fargo.

Then, Wyatt could go and seriously date any of the "approved" women on the list from his mother, and solidify all the pretty money of North Star Capital with the funds of an heiress out of Darlington or Caldwell City.

Wyatt dried his hands on a towel and went to sit by her fireplace. No fire crackled there. *Because he hadn't built one. Wyatt always builds the fires.* Chelsea joined him. Their feet did not share the ottoman.

"Correct me if I'm wrong, but your second question is why I would recommend investing in Cheery Feet, what the numbers mean, so that you can take them to your presentation at North Star Capital and sound—"

"Like I know what I'm talking about?" Wyatt finished her sentence. "I *was* going to ask about Cheery Feet, but not for that reason." He took both her hands. "What I wanted to know was why you would recommend the startup run by none other than Fargo Frye, considering whatever it is that passed between you."

Ah, there he went, referring to his first question again, the one she'd deflected. *Well, I'm not going to tell him all of that. Not today, and probably not ever.* She couldn't revisit it and stay afloat. "The numbers added up."

"It was solely about numbers?"

"Isn't that what North Star Capital is about?" Profits, profits, profits. "Don't forget, I've met Drusilla North on several occasions."

"About my mom …" Wyatt hunched forward, his elbows on his knees. "I had a heart-to-heart talk with her."

Which would imply the woman had a heart. News to Chelsea. "And?"

"And she's not going to be the frozen Mrs. North to you anymore."

"Seriously?" That was wildly improbable. "On what grounds can you say such a thing?" Mrs. North had been systematically icing Heath for a decade, and Chelsea by association—with that night last week being the worst freeze-out ever, by far.

"On the grounds that I finally know what created her grudge against the Sutherlands. And you're not going to believe this, but it involves your uncle Zeke."

"Uncle Zeke!" No way. Suddenly, she was all ears. Chelsea sat back in her chair and tugged the nearest throw blanket over her lap. "Okay, you've got me. Tell me the story, please."

Wyatt detailed the world's most unexpected tragic romance—between his mom, the iciest popsicle this side of the North Pole, and the flightiest bird/blackest sheep in the whole Sutherland family. "When Zeke dumped her, she was so astounded, she … snapped. Decided to hold it against all things Sutherland and Sugarplum Falls forevermore."

Unbelievable. All Chelsea could do was blink. "I can't believe it, but I have to. Because it's too wild for you to have made that up."

"Right?" Wyatt's eyes were wide. The energy between them crackled like old times. "And after she told me the story, she had something she wanted me to give to you."

"A gift? From Mrs. North?" Nuh-uh. "What is it?"

"I'll show you after you answer my three questions."

He had her over a barrel. She had to know what a gift from Mrs. North could be.

150

"All right, but go easy on me." Chelsea steeled herself. "To answer question number two, I guess I have to answer question number one first."

"But I didn't ask you question number one."

"It's about why I freaked out the other night. The real reason."

Wyatt tilted his head to the side. "More or less." Which meant he also wanted to know about Fargo.

She cleared her throat. *It's going to be fine. Wyatt has been my closest friend, whether or not I was furious with him for supposedly taking advantage of me. I can trust him with this story.*

"But don't go telling anyone about this, okay?"

Wyatt nodded gravely. Good, he was taking it seriously. *He takes my feelings seriously.*

Deep breath, and she launched. "Fargo Frye was on the basketball team at Darlington State. When we started dating, I was a statistics tutor, and he needed help passing his stats class so that he could get into business school. He'd just broken up with a girl, one of the basketball cheerleaders, and for the first few times we dated, he claimed I was helping him heal. We spent a lot of time together."

Kissing sessions included.

"We went out here and there like on hikes or bowling, but we spent most of our time at the college library in one of the study rooms, where I was helping him with his homework." And his heart after the breakup, or so Chelsea had thought at the time. "There were a lot of problems he didn't understand, but I showed him how to do all of them. Eventually, he brought his grade up to an A in the class, from failing, just in time to submit his application to business school, right before Christmas."

Wyatt frowned. "He used you."

"It gets worse. I got called into the academic ethics office. They nearly revoked my enrollment. They said I was cheating for him."

"Cheating! You?" Wyatt shook his head. "Of all the people on this earth, you are the last person I could imagine as a cheater."

"They gave me provisional status as a student, and they let me finish my last semester that spring, and graduate, but the black mark on my record kept me out of the graduate program I'd applied to." No master's degree. No PhD in mathematics that would have let her choose a different career besides constant number crunching about medical research she did not have any passion for. She liked it enough, but it didn't light her fire, like being the researcher proper would have done. Fargo hadn't just taken her self-esteem, he'd stolen her career.

"Fargo, on the other hand, did get into a grad program."

"Fargo's parents were major donors to Darlington State, among other places and causes and political candidates." About the only place they hadn't splashed their money was into Fargo's original startup last year. "He was safe. Money protected him."

"That's why you moved home to Sugarplum Falls."

"To work from home, and wear ..." She tugged at the fabric of her Gray Sweats of Shame. "So, in case you thought I had no excuse."

"I never thought that, Chelsea. I just could never have imagined how legitimate it was."

"But, wait. There's more." He hadn't heard the half of it. "The day he got his acceptance letter to MBA school, I thought we were going to dinner to celebrate his victory *and* that he was going to propose to me."

"Propose!"

"Yeah, I was pretty blind. Instead of a proposal of a life together forever, he said some truly cruel things." Which, looking back, she'd been crazy to expect anyway. Fargo had never once brought up the idea of forever. It had all been in Chelsea's mind.

Ha. Kind of like the fake, temporary relationship with Wyatt she'd foolishly dreamed into a long-term relationship.

"Jerk," Wyatt muttered.

"Worse, the next thing I knew, he went back to his blonde little cheerleader girlfriend, who I found out he'd been seeing all along, while he was supposedly dating me. She'd consented to it. In fact, it may have been her idea."

"If it doesn't hurt too much, tell me what cruel things he said," he asked with a murderous blaze in his eye. "I'd like to know, so I can refute them all.

To you and to his face."

Ouch? No. "There are too many, all demeaning." Chelsea couldn't repeat them, except maybe the one. "But I will say this—that he told me I'd never be worthy of receiving a diamond from any guy."

Wyatt flumped backward in his chair, his feet hitting the floor when they fell off the ottoman. "What kind of a ...? I'll smash him."

"Not necessary. He's marrying Esther, remember? He's going to get his fair share of smashing no matter what, beginning tomorrow, until death do them part." Sutherlands didn't get divorced. Other than Uncle Zeke. Except, had he even married all those five women, or had they been common-law marriages? Hard to say with Uncle Zeke.

Several things dawned on Chelsea. One was that she didn't care about Fargo's opinion anymore. Not even a tiny bit. Describing aloud what had happened actually helped it shrink to a manageable size in her heart. *I should have talked about it earlier.*

Another was that Wyatt came to her defense. Like, instantly. In fact, he'd sounded a little like Heath in that moment.

Which pointed a big neon arrow straight at her biggest realization: Wyatt North was nothing like Fargo Frye. In fact, he never had been, and never could be.

Actually, Wyatt was the last person on earth who would deliberately manipulate and hurt her. It wasn't even in his nature.

Wyatt isn't Fargo. He didn't mean to hurt me. Mack spoke the truth.

Chelsea owed Wyatt an apology—again. But not right this second.

"Will you excuse me for a few minutes?" Suddenly Chelsea felt a need to change out of the gray sweats. The manicotti had hit her system, and she had more energy than she'd felt in a while. Plus, she needed a few minutes to collect her thoughts. "I'll answer your next two questions, but can I shower and change first?"

"Sure." Wyatt helped her to her feet. "I have a lot of thoughts I need to work through, and they all involve maiming Fargo Frye. I'll try to get them out of my system."

"Not by acting on them!"

"Who do you think I am, your brother?"

No, he wasn't Heath, either. "So, do you want to … hang around? And I'll be out in a few?"

Please say yes. Chelsea wanted to tell him, but she wanted to feel and look better before she explained the answer to his next question, or what she hoped his next question would be. She needed to be some kind of fierce warrior woman, and needed to look the part in order to play the part.

"As long as you don't mind if I set up another Scrabble game for us."

Chapter 24

Wyatt

Wyatt paced the cottage.

That useless pile of garbage! Fargo Frye deserved to be strung up by his toenails, or any other form of medieval torture, until he saw the error of his ways.

But how much better was Wyatt? Wyatt had allowed Chelsea to face Fargo multiple times, when she should have been shielded—whisked off to some exotic island, rather than get roped into running into him at this series of wedding festivities!

Okay, and what about her family? Huh? How could her family have allowed that? Didn't they know?

They probably didn't know.

The plain fact was, if Heath had known, then Fargo probably would be walking his bride down the aisle courtesy of a wheelchair, thanks to his two broken femurs.

I should have protected her. Of course, Wyatt hadn't known either, so he'd been just as guilty of throwing her to the wolves as everyone else.

The manicotti was not sitting well. His face was hot and pinging. Or maybe it was the anger coursing through his veins.

Wyatt couldn't let Chelsea go another day in this world believing even the slightest amount that she wasn't worthy of the world's *nicest* and biggest diamond. *If I could get my hands on the Hope Diamond right now, it'd belong to Chelsea in two seconds, just to prove it to her.*

"I'll be out in about thirty seconds," Chelsea called from the back room, after her hairdryer shut off. "Sorry for making you wait."

Wyatt quickly rearranged the words he'd placed strategically on the Scrabble board to read *FORGIVE ME*. No, not even a message as strong as a

155

thirty-eight-point-phrase across the double-word score square would suffice. He was going to have to go for the big guns.

"Take your time. Waiting is no problem." Really, it wasn't. Being in Holly Berry Cottage was never a problem. It was always comfort and peace and warmth, even without a fire in the grate. "I'm ready for your answers, though, whenever you're ready to give them to me."

Out walked Chelsea, wearing the burgundy dress with the black velvet sash. "I'm ready."

Yes, she was. For anything. To kill, even. Or at least to ruin Fargo with regret at rejecting all that gorgeousness.

Uh, I'm ready, too. To kiss you senseless. Wyatt couldn't take his eyes off her in that dress. Everything about her was perfectly gorgeous. It was all he could do not to launch himself at her. "That's the dress you were going to wear to the wedding."

"Yeah. It's tonight, isn't it?"

"Uh-huh, but we don't actually have to go to that event, do we?" *We could stay here, and you could model that dress for me, and ...*

"She's my cousin."

"And you're a Sutherland. And Sutherlands show up for each other."

"Even for Esther." She touched her neck. "I forgot something."

Yeah, even for the harder-to-love members of the family. All the Sutherlands accepted Zeke and even let him perform a wedding ceremony. Likewise, Ike and Iris Sutherland allowed the snotty, stuck-up cousin and her terrible fiancé to have their wedding in the family home, even after the puke was bratty to their daughter.

Moreover, they put up with Heath's domineering quirks, trusting that marriage and fatherhood would someday mature him into something mellow, but strong and great.

Best of all, they embraced their son's best friend as a surrogate son, even when he'd shown very little promise there in the principal's office—and they welcomed him with open arms when he declared his love for their daughter, in spite of *still* showing, outwardly, insufficient promise.

They were nurturers. They allowed people to *come as you are.* And loved them.

I want to be a Sutherland. But more than that, he wanted to be with a Sutherland, one special one who made him a better North.

Just now, he wanted to convince her she wanted that too.

"You said your mom had a gift for me?" She stepped back into the living room, this time wearing a pretty necklace and earrings for the first time in ages.

"Wow." Wyatt scraped his jaw off the floor. "Chelsea, you are … wow."

"You're not half bad yourself." She smiled shyly. "Was there a gift?"

Yes, there was. If he could collect himself. "I want to do this right. Better. All of that." He was getting discombobulated. She did that to him. "I could quote you some lyrics, like from 'Winter Wonderland,' because you never get tired of Christmas music, no matter how many times we sing those songs."

"I always like Christmas music."

"Or I could make you a special cup of cocoa with a sprinkle of ginger."

"Even though you hate ginger?"

"No, because you love ginger."

"What is this about, Wyatt?"

"The gift I want to give you, is this." Wyatt dropped to one knee.

Chapter 25

Chelsea

The most shocking moment of her day, and there had been a few, unfolded before her eyes.

Wyatt North, her longtime crush, dropped to one knee. "Chelsea Sutherland?"

Her vocal cords were paralyzed, so she just nodded quickly, her eyes wide and her breath bated.

"You make me the man I am really meant to become. I have loved you for a long time, even when outside forces pressed the pause button—you were always there, residing in my hopes."

She was? Really? "Wyatt," she managed to whisper. *You were in my hopes, too.* But she didn't interrupt, just clenched her hands as though to hold onto the moment and never let it slip away.

"We harmonize. I want us to be a duet—from now on. Not just a Christmas duo, but a New Year's duo, a Valentine's Day duo, every holiday and every day in between. Will you be my wife?" He reached inside the pocket of his suit coat and pulled out the ring she'd returned to him, still as sparkling as before. Except, now, he'd given it to her with the world's most loaded question.

"You mean—" A million endings to that question danced through her mind: *You mean you love me?* was the correct one.

"I mean it. All of it." He held it out to her, and her fist uncurled. She lifted her hand palm down, spreading her fingers so that he could slide the enormous and beautiful, and *real* diamond onto her hand. *The world will know I belong to him.*

"Yes, Wyatt," she managed to whisper. "If you really think I'm worth it."

"Please, Chelsea, you're the one taking the enormous risk here. I don't have the track record to prove that I'm the man you deserve, but I'll spend every day for the rest of my life working to show you that your gamble has paid good dividends." He walked her to the loveseat and kissed her until she couldn't breathe, until she couldn't remember why he wasn't ever at her side, until she couldn't imagine a single day ever passing again without his kiss.

"Thank you for the gift." She leaned her head against his chest, sitting on the sofa, watching the snow sparkle as it fell outside the window of Holly Berry Cottage. "Not to be weird, but did you say there was a gift from your mom?"

Wyatt fidgeted a moment. "About that." He explained how his mom had demanded he return the ring. "When she and I had our heart-to-heart about your uncle Zeke, she finally admitted she'd been judging you through the lens of Zeke's rejection. She told me, *you'd better not let her get away.* But please don't tell her I shared all that with you."

"It'll be our secret." Sharing secrets with Wyatt North was the most delicious thing all day, and that was including the manicotti. "I do love you, Wyatt North. I have ever since ..."

"Ever since when?"

"Ever since I can remember."

"That's your gift to me, then." He pressed a kiss to her head, and then to her temple. His aftershave was perfect at this close range, and it drenched her senses, igniting her desires for his kisses, and more.

But she'd better keep those instincts corralled. Sutherlands believed in keeping certain things just for marriage. *That will be my real gift to Wyatt.*

He lifted her fingers and twisted the ring so that the diamond caught the light. Its spark was a rainbow of fire.

"Forgive me for this, but I'm still kind of having a hard time believing that your mom wanted me to have your ring."

"She was very insistent, at least after I told her how much I was in love with you, and that no other woman on earth would ever do for me."

Oh, heart! "Including the eligible heiresses on the lists she sent you?"

"Honest truth? I never even read the names. Yours was the only one I needed to know."

Chelsea nestled into his arms, and the clock on the mantel struck time to go. They'd have to head over to Holly Berry Cottage in a few minutes. The wedding would be starting. But something else remained to discuss.

"I didn't ever answer your other question."

"The one about Cheery Feet?" Wyatt drew the infinity symbol over and over again across the back of Chelsea's hand. *Forever.* "Did you recommend it to me as some kind of a test? To see whether I was all about money, or whether I cared about the ethics of the person I was investing in, or to see whether I really *would* stand by my promise to invest in Sugarplum Falls first and foremost when I took my seat on the board at North Star Capital?"

"You're so used to being tested by your parents, I can see how you'd ask this." A little chuckle rose in the back of her throat. "I mean, those would have all been good reasons. But they weren't actually factors. I actually did think his business's numbers looked like they'd give North Star Capital the best return on investment, so I couldn't hide that from you."

"Even though you knew I'd trust your judgment implicitly, and you could have told me anything was best and I'd have taken your word—without even rechecking the math for myself?"

"Seriously? You would have just taken my word for it?"

"Chelsea, you're trustworthy. Therefore, I trust you." There he went, turning on that irresistible charm again. "I can't help myself. You're also the smartest person I know."

"At math, possibly, but what about at Scrabble?" She could never quite beat him.

"Ha. I suspect you let me win some of those so that I won't get discouraged and quit playing."

"Not at all. I stay up nights trying to come up with words to beat you. You see patterns in letters, and language, and in people's behaviors and needs." Which Chelsea could never hope to do.

Now that she recognized it and thought it through, it wasn't just some kind of shallow *charm* Wyatt exuded. It was an ability that he'd long cultivated. A skill to put people at ease and bring out *the happy* in them.

"Look, Wyatt. It may not be math, but what you can do is a gifted-and-talented level of intelligence I can never hope to achieve. I'm in awe of you daily. It's what makes you the most valuable player at your job and … in life."

"Stop it." Wyatt shook his head. "I'm not worthy of any of that."

"Are you kidding?" Chelsea wanted to shake him. He couldn't actually be denying these truths, shrugging them off as if she were offering false flattery. "Please. You're going to be that investment firm's star."

"Please. I'd love to believe what you're saying, but let's be real. My parents and the members of the board at North Star Capital will never see it like that. I don't do the math, so I am nothing but dead weight."

"But you bring in the clients. They can't resist your magnetism." And neither could Chelsea. Or her family. Or anyone Wyatt ever encountered. "Give it some time, you'll show them."

"I'm not investing in Cheery Feet. Not if it's Fargo Frye." Wyatt shook his head. "I have always had a gut feeling against novelty socks, even before he started Jingle Toes back in the day. Despite the numbers. Despite the pressure from my parents."

"Your parents were steering you toward Cheery Feet? Did they know it belonged to Fargo?"

"Actually, I can't figure out why. Unless they ran all the data ahead of time, too." He smirked. "More of their testing."

"I might know why they were pushing for it. Fargo comes from a big financial powerhouse family in Caldwell City. They own Sierra Investments."

"Sierra Investments? Really?"

"Yeah, you've heard of them, right? Real estate developers, shipping, a whole tech sector as well."

"Heard of them! My parents practically worship at the Sierra Investments altar." Wyatt drummed his finger on her arm. "You're saying Fargo belongs to that family? Isn't their last name Frei?"

"Frye, Frei, it's the same name, different spellings."

"It sounds like you know this already, but Sierra Investments is a huge conglomerate. It manages all the stuff you listed, plus Caldwell General Hospital, as well as an airplane manufacturing company, and a dozen car dealerships out on the coast." Wyatt pressed the heel of his hand into his forehead. "All the things on the list were related."

"Through Sierra Investments?"

"Exactly." He smacked the center of his forehead. "No wonder my parents were pushing me to invest in Cheery Feet."

"Of course they were. It's a potentially great return on investment. The numbers look stellar, and a huge percentage of the company could be bought with a relatively small sum, compared with the ROI from the others you sent ."

"No, no." Wyatt huffed and his eyes went wide. "It's like you said—the best way to win someone's affection is to be kind to their kids. Fargo's the owner of Cheery Feet. My mom and dad wanted me to get to the Frei family's hearts by buttering up their kid."

"Are you sure?"

Wyatt pinched the bridge of his nose. "Mack told me—look into ownership. Look deeper." He growled. "I can't believe I didn't look deeper. I'm not investing there."

"Don't do that out of some kind of misguided loyalty to me, Wyatt. You've got a lot of different hats you have to wear. Obviously, I'd rather you didn't end up bankrolling my evil ex, but if it's the right thing to do for North Star Capital, then be wise. Do what has to be done."

"I'm telling you, my gut says no." Wyatt shook his head. "I haven't got the number crunching skills like you, or like my mom or dad, but I do have instincts. You said so yourself."

Chelsea nodded. "I trust them." It didn't make sense on paper, but she agreed," Go with that."

"I still have to invest. They want me to report on Monday morning. First thing." Wyatt's temple pulsed, as did his jaw muscles. "Something else is going to turn up."

"Something that isn't on the list?" *Trust him. Support him. He's not playing.* "You can do this, Wyatt."

"I know I can. With your help." He looked up at the clock. "We missed the actual ceremony, I'm afraid. Should we also skip the after-party?"

No. Not a chance. Chelsea was going to make an appearance at this wedding, no matter what.

Chapter 26

Wyatt

A Sutherland wedding reception put on at Holly Berry House was not to be missed in Sugarplum Falls. Or so it would seem by the jam-packed crowd.

And the pure chaos.

By the time Wyatt and Chelsea walked in holding hands, post nuptials, the whole of Holly Berry House was in an uproar. Kaden and Jaidyn were rehearsing their songs for the town Christmas play at the tops of their lungs. Ike Sutherland had an entire roomful of former students' parents in stitches over his storytelling—insider secrets of a principal's life as a disciplinarian over kid pranks.

Then there was the bride.

"These canapés were supposed to be *Greek* flavored, not Italian." She stomped her foot at Mario himself. "I knew I should have ordered my catering straight out of Darlington and not trusted it to the local yokels."

The mayoral mother of the bride reached around Esther's neck and placed a cupping hand over the bride's mouth. "Sweetheart, this is your day as a queen. Act like a queen, not a court jester."

A strangling scream came from behind the hand-gag.

Wyatt tugged Chelsea along through the crowd, but the mayor dropped her chore of muzzling her daughter and came to greet them.

"Well, we missed you earlier, but if I were newly engaged, I'd be late to everything else, too." She winked exaggeratedly. "It's amazing how each time I see you, Chelsea, you just get more and more stunning. I'm no math whiz, but I'd call it *exponential*."

"And I'd agree," Wyatt interrupted before Chelsea could object. "Did you get a chance to see her ring? We're looking at a winter wedding, too."

"Here at Holly Berry House as well?" Mayor Lang asked. "Because this is the home Chelsea grew up in, and the acoustics are grand, as you well know, especially in the foyer where the piano sits beneath the grand staircase. I mean, a wedding duet with the bride and groom performing? It's not often done, but I can feel it already."

Wow. So his wedding program was already being detailed by Chelsea's aunt Lisa. *I'd better get used to it.* "Sounds really nice."

"I'm so happy to see you two as a duet rather than a trio, by the way. Duets are so much cozier. They are the beginnings of important things." She winked again.

"Thanks for your kindness, Aunt Lisa. Would you like to see the ring?" Chelsea held out her hand graciously. "It was Wyatt's grandmother's ring. It's special."

Aunt Lisa gasped.

Wyatt might as well get used to calling her that now, instead of just Mayor Lang.

"Oh, my stars! That is a serious diamond. It's a thousand times more valuable than that fakey-fake my fabulous but cheap son-in-law planted on Esther's finger. But you're worth it, Chelsea." Aunt Lisa pinched Chelsea's cheek. "You know how to pick good ones."

"Thanks," Chelsea said.

"Thanks," Wyatt echoed, since it was a compliment for him, too.

They wandered through the crowd. Up walked Aunt Rita and Uncle Lester.

Aunt Rita held a hand at her heart. "Oh, Chelsea, darling. You look like a dream! Upstaging the bride at her own wedding isn't polite, you know."

"Oh, you're so sweet, Aunt Rita." Chelsea blushed modestly. "Esther is a pretty bride."

"But you're a gorgeous fiancée of an equally gorgeous man." Aunt Rita ran her eyes down Wyatt's frame one time—approvingly. "And from what I hear, he's not just charming and handsome. He's also a future vice president of North Star Capital."

More guests thronged through, cutting off the conversation, and leaving

Wyatt to wonder, *Where did she hear that?*

Up walked Mack. "Dude. I'm telling everyone the great news, but maybe I should have checked with you first."

"Which news is that?"

"North Star Capital sent out a press release naming you vice president, starting January one. They must have liked your recommendation."

But ... he hadn't even made a recommendation yet. Stymieing. And yet—was it in his reach?

"Come with me." Chelsea pulled Wyatt up the grand staircase to a landing that overlooked the foyer. "We can breathe a little better up here."

"Breathing is good." Wyatt threaded his fingers between hers. "It's not overrated. Nor is kissing you." He pressed his lips to her temple. "To clarify, I don't know whether I'm a future vice president at my parents' firm. This is the first I've heard of it."

"Whether or not you are, I don't really care. You're someone who will be successful in any field you choose. You don't have to be confined to North Star Capital just because it's a family business."

No? Wyatt blinked for a second, letting that sink in. Forever he'd just assumed that was going to be his route in life: mess around until he was done messing around, and then settle in at the family firm. It was what girl after girl he'd dated had pried out of him as his eventual future, and probably why several had chased him harder than a starving fox chases a rabbit in the winter.

If I marry Chelsea, she won't have those same expectations. She'll let me do whatever suits me best. She'd support him.

I can succeed in whatever I do choose.

All the same, he wanted to know why the announcement had been made. "Can I just check something?" He looked in his phone, and sure enough, there were several emails. One, the press release. Another, a message from the company congratulating him. *How personal.* Finally, there was actually a personal note from his mom.

Son, I have done a lot of soul-searching since we talked. Your insights made me realize several things. For now, I'll say that one of them is North Star Capital needs someone exactly like you. To keep us grounded, rooted in our history so we don't lose it. Your dad and I are proud of you for the good man you've become. I hope you accept the promotion, and we hope you'll use the position to create strong ties with our local community.

Wyatt turned off his screen and let his arm hang limp.

"What? Is everything okay?" Chelsea asked.

"They want me to be …"

"Vice president?" Chelsea prompted after a long moment's pause.

He nodded then shook his head. How could he put it? "Yes, and *myself.*"

Chelsea threw her arms around his neck. "That's wonderful!" She kissed his cheek and he hugged her to him. Wyatt enfolded her, the woman who made it all hap—

"Stop it." A woman's angry voice floated up into the foyer's rafters above them. "Stop it right now, Mr. Frye. I'm here to serve hors d'oeuvres and refill water glasses, not to have you grope me."

Down below, beneath the curving staircase where the piano usually sat, a melodrama was playing out. Chelsea and Wyatt leaned over the balcony just enough to see.

Fargo begged in a sloshy voice, "Come on, Amber. We could have something special." He hooked a finger into the front of her shirt and then attempted to undo the top button.

"We only dated once." She jerked out of his grasp and redid her button. "You got married an hour ago."

"Right? So I should be on my honeymoon. Let's go." But it was more like *let 'sh goh.* Drunken, sorry, and despicable. "Baby!" He lunged at her, his hands aiming for places he shouldn't grab on anyone but his new wife.

"I'd better go help." Wyatt left the landing, ready to channel his inner Heath and stop the assault, but Chelsea caught his sleeve.

"I think that girl can handle herself." Chelsea pointed. "Look."

At the bottom of the stairs, Amber stormed past, yanking her apron off and throwing it on the floor. She hollered over her shoulder at the front door, "I don't have to take this. Not for minimum wage. You're a jerk." The front door slammed.

Yikes. "Looks like we'd better warn your mom about a pending

166

harassment case."

"Yeah." Chelsea heaved a sigh. "Thank you for saving me from that." She aimed a thumb at the drunken Fargo stumbling off toward the living room and calling for Esther.

"What? I didn't save you from that. You did." Except, maybe Wyatt *had* done something right by stepping into the fake-became-real boyfriend role just in time to keep her from wishing after Fargo ever again. "Thank you for giving me the chance. You're pretty amazing, Chelsea." He took her hand and held out her fingers, the ring glinting in the chandelier's light from above.

Wyatt looked at Chelsea. "There's no way *that dude* is getting a penny from North Star Capital. My gut *and* my brain say no to Cheery Feet."

"Yeah, people can just order their puppy-face socks from catalogs!" she called over the balcony to no one in particular.

"Like Chelsea does!" Wyatt hollered, too.

"Wyatt!" She whirled on him. "How did you—?"

"Chelsea, the catalog with the puppy-face socks had your name on it, not your grandma's. And I saw the socks. They're cute."

"Wyatt? Reading other people's mail is a federal offense."

"No, stealing it is. And trust me. I absolutely didn't steal that catalog. I told you, I don't get a good feeling about novelty socks."

"What you should trust is your gut. *And* your brilliant brain."

"Brilliant." Pah.

"You always beat me at Scrabble."

"You always *let* me beat you at Scrabble."

"Are we back to this again? Please. Absolutely not." Chelsea shook her head. "I'm giving our Scrabble games my letter-best."

"I see what you did there."

"The point is, Wyatt"—Chelsea drew a circle on his skin with her fingertip, sending him to Tingleville—"that we each have strengths. When we're together, we combine them. We're a product of our strengths, not our weaknesses. Two positives multiplied result in a greater positive. Two negatives, our weaknesses, when multiplied also result in a positive outcome— because we'll have each other."

"In other words, you'll do the math, and I'll be the first to initiate conversations with our neighbors?" He wouldn't have to be the weak link in the North family *we're numbers people* chain anymore. He'd have a bolstering power at his side.

"Precisely." She smiled up at him, her smile like all the stars in the night sky combined. "I'm sorry I freaked out."

"You had a right to."

"Will you let me make it up to you by double checking your math-facts at work from now on?"

He certainly would. He leaned in for a kiss, but a voice interrupted it.

"Excuse me, is this a party for two?" Beau Cabot stood at the bottom of the stairs. "I'm looking for Wyatt."

"It's me, Beau." He called over the balcony and pulled Chelsea to his side. "I'm here with Chelsea."

"Nice to finally track you down." Beau was more relaxed than when they'd run into him with his rambunctious kids at the Hot Cocoa Festival a few weeks ago. "I'm here on behalf of Tazewell Solutions." The military software company was headquartered in Sugarplum Falls, and when Beau wasn't corralling kids, he was chairing the board there.

"Tazewell needs me?" He came down the stairs and shook Cabot's outstretched hand. "I know precious little about the military, and even less about software. But how can I help?"

"Can I speak confidentially?"

Oh. Wyatt sobered. "Of course. Can Chelsea stay? I get it if this needs to be a private meeting."

"No, it's fine. Chelsea is trustworthy." He looked at his spit-shined shoes and then back up at Wyatt, his gaze boring into Wyatt's like a thousand lives depended on what he said next. "Tazewell Solutions is in trouble. We need a cash infusion to tide us over on payroll until Christmas. I'm asking you to take a risk, in exchange for a percentage of the shares I own in the company. I can't guarantee anything, since it's all out of my hands. In fact, your investment could turn to dust. But I don't think it will. I think … I think you'll be a very happy man, come the end of December."

168

"Tell me more," he said aloud, but Wyatt's gut told him everything he needed to know.

Chapter 27

Chelsea

"Chelsea! There you are!" Mom found Chelsea and Wyatt as they were finishing up their discussion with Beau Cabot, just as Wyatt shook hands on a deal. A good deal. "The crowd is clamoring for a song from Christmas Tree-O."

Wyatt said good night to a very relieved-looking Beau Cabot, and they left for the front room, with Mom chatting all the way.

"I've been looking for Heath for an hour, but I can't find either him *or* Odessa. It's like they had as bad of a time at this awful wedding party as the bride and groom themselves. You've got to come and save the evening before the 'happy' couple scratch each other's eyes out, and the rest of the guests mutiny."

Where could Heath have gone? Dang it! "We can sing, Mom, but if they're wanting the trio, that's not going to work."

"They'll be happy to have the duo. Just *do* something. Quick." She broke into a jog, heading through to the main family living area. "Decide what you're going to sing. I'll try to keep down the angry mob."

Angry mob! Just what had been going on at Holly Berry House? It wasn't a usual destination for angry mobs.

She turned to Wyatt. He looked more amused than worried. *Pure Wyatt.* "What about something beautiful—and calm—like you?"

They found their spot at the microphone. Luckily, Mom sat at the piano with her big *Reader's Digest Merry Christmas Songbook* at the ready.

"Page one hundred seventy-two, Mom." Chelsea cleared her throat and found her note as soon as Mom started playing the left hand's distinct, rolling chords for "O Holy Night." The crowd quieted instantly. In this song, there was no back-and-forth between Wyatt and Chelsea, no push or pull. Just a harmony.

Everyone was listening, and when it was over, someone begged for an old standby from their repertoire, "The Christmas Song."

Mom obliged by turning to page forty-seven, playing the familiar complex chords that led to the lyrics about chestnuts. Chelsea took the line that killed her every time: "Everybody knows a turkey ..."

She certainly did. Fargo Frye was the biggest turkey of all time. Hands down.

But then again, Fargo's reentry into her life had changed everything. Spurred her and Wyatt into action, and into love. They might not have found it without that turkey. *I have the man I love. He found the perfect place to invest his capital. We're together in Holly Berry House with the people I love most in the world.*

When his verse came, Wyatt sang as if Chelsea were the only person in the room. He held her hand and sang straight to her heart about tiny tots.

Then came the harmony verse, offering a simple phrase, to kids of all ages. They sang, their voices blending like they'd been singing together for years. Like they could sing together forever, just the two of them, and it would be enough.

"Merry Christmas, to you," came the final words—and then Wyatt pulled both microphones aside and kissed Chelsea full on the mouth, in full view of everyone. Then he pulled away with a *whoop!* "That's the girl I love! That's the girl I'm going to marry!"

The crowd applauded, shouting congratulations. Wyatt held Chelsea's left hand aloft and showed off the ring to the whole assembly, grinning like he'd won life's lottery.

I'm the winner here.

No, they both were.

"Chelsea." Up marched Esther, grabbing her by the arm and jerking her into the hallway where just a few nights ago, Fargo had bothered Chelsea.

"When will you *stop*?" Esther's white gown flounced as she stomped her foot.

"Stop what? My mom is the one who asked us to sing. I assume you're the one who put Christmas Tree-O on your program, since it's your wedding day."

"Not that. The singing is ... *whatever*." Her highly eye-shadowed eyes rolled. "I mean ... Ugh. I don't know what I mean, but I'm so sick and tired of you." Her voice cracked.

The feeling is more than mutual, I assure you. "Esther, it's your wedding day. Emotions are running high. What about cutting the cake with Fargo now?"

Esther let out a growl that turned into a scream. Wyatt peeked his head in, catching Chelsea's eye, but she gave him a *not yet* shake of her head, and he backed away.

I have this.

"Esther, I don't really know what's going on here. Did I offend you tonight?"

"You have been offending me since we were eleven and you started thinking of yourself as so much better than me. Too cool to be my friend anymore."

Um, where was this coming from? "I have no idea what you're talking about. You're the one who started wearing the latest fashions, listening to *cool* music, and talking about hair and boys all the time. I am the one who did math homework. Which of us was cool?"

"That's exactly what I'm talking about. You were better at school. Better at math. Better at boys."

Better at boys? Shah! As if. "What on earth are you talking about?"

"You had Heath as your older, cool brother. Which meant you got to hang out with *Wyatt North* every day of your life. In what universe does that not equate to cooler?"

"You dropped me as your cousin-friend, Esther."

"Because you dropped me as yours. I couldn't bother hoping to become the valedictorian because you already were. I couldn't become a great singer in the town's most beloved trio because you already were. I couldn't be a mathematics genius or a chestnut-haired beauty who looked like a Barbie doll come to life because you were already filling those slots. Even my own mother told me a thousand times, 'Why can't you be more like your cousin Chelsea?' Chelsea this, Chelsea that. I can never live up. Even when I chase and date and *marry* your cast-off boyfriend, I'm not enough."

Whoa. A thousand realizations slammed together, like a traffic accident, one car rear-ending the one in front, over and over. *She was jealous. She wanted everything I had, even Fargo.*

"Esther." Chelsea opened her arms and took the messy, weeping, mascara-smudged bride into an embrace. "I had no idea you felt any of these things."

Esther's shoulders shook, and she took a long, sniffling breath. "You went off to be in the trio, and I was alone. All I could do was hair. And act like a witch to everyone I meet."

"But you do hair like a rock star." She probably actually did the hair *of* rock stars, if rumors were true about Esther's confidential client list. The witchiness was at stellar levels, too. "I could never do that. I couldn't put together a fashionable outfit if I tried."

Esther snorted. "Come on. Look at what you're wearing. It's like you stepped out of a magazine."

"People from a boutique over in Reindeer Crossing chose every item of clothing I have on. Other people have to dress me for me not to look like a slug." Was Chelsea really having this conversation? "But, hey. Two things, Esther." She pulled away and gave Esther a serious look. These were two serious things. "Listen carefully."

Esther wiped her eyes and sniffed. "Okay."

"First, your mother, who I adore, was wrong—*totally wrong*—to compare you to me. I don't care what it was about. That was an error in her parenting judgment. But her love for you knows no bounds, whether or not she made that mistake. She's insanely proud of what you've made of yourself. To the point of the rest of us tuning it out as she breaks into bragging spells on a regular basis."

Esther blinked for a second, leaving little black brush marks below her eyes again. "Really?" she asked, her voice as soft as Chelsea had ever heard it.

"She is?"

"A hundred percent."

After a long moment of silence, it appeared Esther was letting Chelsea's words sink in, take root, and grow. "I want to believe you so much."

"Then do. And listen. Whatever strangeness was in our past, let's put it behind us. It happened, but it's not happening, and it doesn't matter. We can look forward, you and I. More than anything I'd love for us to be close again. With no comparisons." Please, no comparisons. "You can be great in your ways of being great, and I'll try to do my thing, as well."

Slowly, Esther nodded, but now the tears were coming down in broad sheets, making her cheeks reminiscent of Sugarplum Falls. Maybe some of the bitterness was flowing out, too, and the witch-persona would starve to death without it. Someday. Maybe not immediately.

"Stay right here a sec. I haven't said the second thing." Chelsea dashed to the buffet, snagged a pile of white napkins, and dashed back, where she handed them to Esther. "And this second thing is even more vital to your happiness."

"What's that?"

"Fargo Frye is ..." How could Chelsea put it truthfully but delicately.

"A toad. I know it." Forget the delicacy, then.

"And you married him anyway?" That was just crazy.

Esther gulped visibly and looked at the ceiling. "I thought ... I thought if he was good enough for you to break your heart over, he must be something special. When he noticed me, I fell for his—I can't exactly call it charm." She shook her head. "His façade. Yeah. And the fact his family owned Sierra Investments. Which I totally shouldn't have been blinded by, since I'm a Sutherland, but I was."

"You don't have to stay married to him."

"But I said *I do*."

"Yes, but if you really don't, it's okay to change your mind."

"Sutherlands don't get divorced."

"Which is why it's better to take care of the cancellation now, this minute, than to wait and have to divorce him." When Esther looked confused, Chelsea explained. "*Annulment.* You can get one easily since you haven't even

174

been on the honeymoon yet. I think Andrew Kingston was here tonight."

"One of the family that owns the orchard?" Esther looked confused.

"Yes, but he's an attorney, and we can ask him, and you can head to his office first thing Monday morning. Meanwhile, I think there could be police cars here in the next few minutes to pick up your groom."

"Police cars!"

With a grudging honesty, Chelsea explained the *Amber, baby, come on* moment beneath the stairs, as well as Amber's threats to file charges.

"So you didn't break your heart over him? He wasn't someone worth it?"

"I did break my heart over him, but that doesn't automatically mean he was worth it." She might as well come clean to Esther, and she told her all about the way Fargo used her, and the hideous breakup.

Esther looked horrified. "No wonder you were heartsick."

Sick was right. "Because he used me so badly, my pride was hurt most, and then my self-worth. And then my career was gone, too, so it felt like my whole future. I guess it just spilled into my heart."

Now it was Esther's turn to hug Chelsea. "I wish I'd been there for you. I'm so sorry for my jealousy. I guess I wanted to be the one singing with you and Heath and Wyatt. I do sing, you know."

"Tell you what." Chelsea didn't break the hug. "With Heath gone, we'd love to have someone else sing lead in Christmas Tree-O. If you want to."

"You'd let me? After I've been so awful to you?"

"It's in the past."

Esther slowly shook her head, as if she couldn't believe Chelsea could be kind. "How about this? What if I find someone *not lame* to marry, someone who likes to sing, and we create a Christmas quartet with Wyatt and you, and Mr. Right and me?"

"Sounds like a real Sutherland family Christmas." And it did.

Esther broke into a laugh. A healing laugh. A laugh that symbolized the real promise of Christmas—that the real gifts are of healed hearts, of mended fences, and of family love.

Chapter 28

Wyatt

"We never did find Heath." Wyatt held Chelsea's hand and walked her toward Holly Berry Cottage, shortly after the police left Holly Berry House and after they'd both given their witness statements to the police. *I didn't expect to make a witness statement at a family wedding when I got up this morning. But I also didn't expect to be engaged to Chelsea again. To have her love me again.* "Where did he and Odessa go?"

"Not sure. But isn't it great about Esther being freed from Fargo's clutches?"

It was probably lucky for both Esther and Fargo. Neither of them was likely to bring out the best in the other, long term. "You two are friends again. That's the greater thing."

"Yeah." Chelsea squeezed his hand, and pulsations of her energy flowed through him. He couldn't get enough of her touch. "She's all right, actually. I just didn't know it. We have some lost time to make up for, but we've got the rest of our lives as cousins. That's one of the great things about families. All the repeat chances when we mess up. It's like we're here in families as a testing ground for learning to forgive and forget."

Wyatt hadn't thought of it that way. *I need to forgive Mom. I think I might be on my way to doing that.* "Christmas is a good time to remember that."

"Christmas is a good time for a lot of things. Like falling in love." Chelsea bent down and scooped up a mitten of powder snow and sprinkled it all over him. "Falling, get it?"

"You little …" Wyatt scooped up a handful of snow and scattered it over her hair and onto her nose and shoulders. She squealed like she was twelve again, and they were having their first snow fight—one of many, many snow fights they'd had over the years of togetherness. "Come here." They were at the porch of Holly Berry Cottage, and Wyatt gathered her into his arms. "Tell me what word you'd spell with the following letters: *I-L-O-V-E-Y-O-U.*"

"That's eight letters. In Scrabble you only get seven."

"Okay, I'll defer, since you're the math person in this relationship." He kissed her cheek, her eyelid, her temple, her lips. She relaxed into his kisses, and he made sure every one of her billion trillion zillion cells knew he meant his Scrabble word from the depths of his heart. The sincerest places.

"I love you, too," Chelsea whispered. "Even if it only gives me sixteen points on the board and you're still ahead by fifty points in our running total."

"I win."

"So do I."

Chapter 29

Chelsea

"I can't believe this is happening so fast!" Chelsea tugged at the bodice of her white gown. "When everyone said long courtship, short engagement, I didn't think it would be *this* short."

"Well, we had all the decorations, dear. And the poinsettias were still alive."

"I did always want poinsettias as my wedding flowers." And everything else—like to have the wedding at Holly Berry House, and to have all the family there, and even to have shrimp canapés as her refreshments.

The dress she wore came from the Crossing Clothiers with a special note from Amélie and Gregor. *We know this is right for you.* And it was. It was perfect. Even better, Chelsea hadn't needed to try on a million dresses and get discombobulated by the decision. Amélie and Gregor were the best. Oh, and she'd found out what the deal was with them and Wyatt. Wyatt had gone to bat for them when they came and asked for an investor to start Crossing Clothiers two years ago, despite Mom and Dad North's insistence that they were minnows not whales.

"Besides"—Mom placed a white floral spray along the edge of the up-do Esther had created of Chelsea's hair—"in the Sutherland family, the longer the courtship, the shorter the engagement should be. There's a direct correlation. Do the math."

Even though, technically, Wyatt and Chelsea had been dating only … whoa. Too short of a time for anyone in today's world to think they were sane for tying the knot, really, they'd been, as Aunt Lisa had said at the bridal shower thrown by Esther, circling each other for a decade.

And the chemistry was much too potent for a long engagement and still

178

be able to have a Sutherland-approved wedding.

"So, what you're saying is since I've been hanging out with Wyatt for a decade, I should be engaged for ten minutes."

"Ten days, dear."

Chelsea started to giggle. "If you hadn't stuck me in the back of the head with that bobby pin so hard, I'd think I was dreaming and needed to wake up."

"He's a gem, Chelsea. We are so happy to finally have you two be happy together. You will make him a wonderful wife. And he'll be so good to you. That's one thing about him I know will be a hundred percent dependable."

Not just good to her, he'd be so good for her, too. "I love him, Mom. Depend on that."

"I've seen that for ages."

She had? "Why didn't you tell me?"

"Would you have believed me?"

Of course not. "Any word from Heath and Odessa?" Due to more labor pains, they'd disappeared from the *Wedding of Terror that Ended with the Police Report* just in time to miss the singing performance and the assault charges excitement. "I know I should be focused on my wedding, but emotionally I'm in full-on baby-watch mode."

"You and me both, sweetie." Mom finished fussing with Chelsea's hair. She gave Chelsea the warmest hug. "This is the best Christmas I could dream of."

Chelsea, too. A knock sounded at the door to Chelsea's old bedroom at Holly Berry House. "Can I come in?"

"Of course, Wyatt." Mom cleared a space for Wyatt at Chelsea's side. "Your bride looks gorgeous. Go ahead and look at her. We don't stand on any *bad luck* hocus-pocus around here."

Wyatt came to Chelsea and took her in his arms. "This is the happiest day of my life." He kissed her on the top of her head. "I'll kiss you more later. How many Scrabble points for the word"—he whispered in her ear in and she giggled.

Mom coughed a little. "I'll just be going."

"No, Mrs. Sutherland." Wyatt dropped his hold on Chelsea. "I came down to find you. Well, both of you."

Uh-oh. What was going on? Chelsea's muscles tensed. "Is something wrong?" Was Mrs. North throwing a fit? Had she changed her mind about letting her precious son marry a Sutherland—after running into Uncle Zeke upstairs? Oh, dear. "Is everything okay?"

"It's more than okay." Wyatt's eyes danced. "I'm an uncle."

Chelsea blinked. Wyatt had no siblings. How could ... "Oh!"

"Yep." He beamed. "I mean, it's technically going to be a half hour or so until I say *I do* and it officially becomes my status, but Heath called Mr. Sutherland a second ago to say that Odessa had a baby girl. Healthy, eight pounds two ounces. They're naming her Holly. After the Holly Berry House."

It was utterly perfect for a Christmas birthday girl.

Chelsea threw her arms around Wyatt. "This is the best day ever!"

Then she ran to Mom. "You're a grandma!"

A tear splashed on Mom's cheek. "I am." Then she broke into a laugh as Chelsea returned to Wyatt's arms. "You know what else is a Sutherland tradition? Upstaging each other's weddings."

Maybe, but Chelsea couldn't possibly mind. Holly was the best wedding gift she could imagine. "Let's go make you an uncle." She grinned up at Wyatt.

Mom left the room, and the door closed on just the almost-bride-and-groom.

"Yes," Wyatt said in a sultry, sexy voice. "And after that, let's go work on making me a dad next."

Okay, so maybe *that* would be the best Christmas gift ever.

Epilogue

Beau Cabot

"Gemma. Why aren't you watching Mac and Adele?" Beau stood in his Air Force Reserve captain's uniform, steam clinging to his lungs, as the young woman he'd assumed would be minding his children circled the natural hot springs pool on the ground level of his home, Turtledove Place. "Where are they?"

Gemma swam her way to the edge and looked up at him with wanton eyes. "They're playing a game. I thought you'd be glad to meet me here, since you're tired from work." She shook her red hair and batted her wet lashes at him in the dim, steamy room.

He was tired from work, but he had another job to go to—right now. "I'm late for my military assignment. The kids need dinner." The first weekend of every month, he was committed to the Reserve, and he'd never been late.

"Come on, Beau. You can't be a workaholic and a daddy *all* the time. Sometimes you've gotta be a man, too." She hoisted her lean figure from the pool, wrapped herself in a towel, and stalked toward him.

"Gemma." Beau backed away from the dripping-wet girl who came at him with that same predatory look as her predecessors. Not all had been as scantily clad as this one, but they'd all sooner or later made advances on him. Gemma acted sooner. *Three weeks. She worked fast.*

"Yes, Beau?" She dropped her towel. "The kids are totally occupied. Wouldn't you like to be occupied as well?"

Beau had places to be. And none of them were in the arms of a vapid

181

culinary school dropout who couldn't even make boxed macaroni and cheese and who let his kids atrophy on screens all day. *About the same as my ex-wife.*

"We could take a swim first, if you want."

The clock on the wall showed he had less than fifteen minutes to get out of the house or be late to his Friday night meeting with the other officers. They'd be expecting Captain Cabot's input, as well as his presentation on troop readiness for their unit. "Get dressed, Gemma."

"Where's the fun in that?"

This got more useless by the minute. His third nanny in five months, he was getting exhausted by the revolving door.

But Gemma was not giving in. "It's such a gorgeous house, Beau. The pool, the view, the hot, lonely guy who owns it. Everything about it is rich. We could be rich together, you know. I'd be really good at it."

Even though the ticking clock demanded that Beau leave his kids in someone's care, and even though he had nowhere else to turn, he clenched his teeth and uttered the defeating words.

"Gemma, you're fired."

"Fired!" the redhead gasped, touching her bare collarbone. "But Beau, I thought ..." She gathered the towel up from the deck. "I thought you hired me for *all* the reasons. Not just for the kids."

"Nope. Goodbye."

Her lower lip shot out. She wrapped the towel around herself and stomped up the stairs toward the nanny quarters on the main floor.

Without Gemma to watch Mac and Adele, he wasn't going to be able to leave for his weekend assignment at the Command Base two hours away from Sugarplum Falls.

Beau rubbed the persistent knot at the top of his spine near his right shoulder. Was there a word in the English language for how tired this year left him? At least it was almost over. If he could just get through December. Most years, December meant holidays. Not this year. This year, it meant his entire weekday career's existence hung in the balance with the survival or death of Tazewell Solutions.

With slow, plodding steps, he climbed the back stairs to his home office

182

on the main floor, where he stayed until he heard Gemma's door slam and her car drive off. He'd have to call them at the base and tell them about his family emergency. *I've never missed a single month's assignment since I transferred from active duty to the Reserve.*

And he shouldn't now, either. There had to be a solution.

Giggles and upbeat music sailed through the air from the living room where the kids were, sure enough, playing a video game.

"Mac, Adele. You want to go see Aunt Elaine?" His late step-father's sister worked with Beau at Tazewell Solutions. Once or twice since Tracey left, Elaine had defended the home front for Beau. "She might want company for the weekend."

Mac and Adele looked up from the video game they'd become far too expert at over the past weeks of Gemma's oversight. If Aunt Elaine was in charge, she'd military-school them right out of video-game mode. Actually, Beau should have been able to do that himself, if only he'd possessed an iota of energy.

"Aw, do we have to?" Mac whined. "She doesn't like us to come over." Was his lisp getting more pronounced? The whine definitely was.

"Yeah, I broke that glass thing last time." Adele was looking at the game again. "She said I couldn't come back until I had learned some manners." Suddenly, she did look up. "Manners. M-a-n-n-e-r-s. I'm the class representative for the spelling bee right before Christmas break." She beamed. Her teeth were too big for her face, and it made her really cute. Her white-blonde hair was just like her mother's. So was Mac's.

Plus, she had a point. Elaine, at sixty, had a very low tolerance level for kid antics. He video dialed her anyway. What choice did he have?

"Elaine. Any chance you'd like to spend the weekend at Turtledove Place?" That, at least, was better than letting the kids wreck her house.

"Beau?" A loud motor wound down in the background. Probably her blender. She was the queen of green smoothies. "You didn't fire your nanny again, did you?"

"She invited me for a swim. Et cetera." The girl might as well have had dollar-signs tattooed on her eyelids.

The whirring sound ended. "That's three since August." She sipped a green smoothie on the screen.

Don't remind me. "Do you have any suggestions for a replacement n-a-n-n-y?"

Adele's head popped up from the game again. "Dad. I'm in the third grade. I can spell *nanny*. I can also spell *dulcimer* and *abstinence,* in case you're interested."

Over the video call screen Elaine raised a brow. "I'm glad they're teaching abstinence in schools these days."

"What's abstinence?" Mac shouted at Beau, shaking his game controller above his head. "Is it better than Santa Claus's aerodynamic sleigh?"

"I can also spell *havoc,*" Adele announced. "That's what Giselle said we wreaked."

"You need help, Beau."

Gemma, Giselle, Gigi. They'd been no help at all.

"Give me the weekend and I'll have someone permanent." Probably. Why did his clothes suddenly feel like they were lined with lead? "Are there any elderly widows in the Sugarplum Falls Historical Society who'd like to earn a little extra money?" He hadn't searched for help from anyone in that age range yet.

"Good nannies are hard to come by. What you need is a wife." Elaine picked up the tall glass of dark green liquid. "What about that nice Olympia Barron? She's single and attractive. On the bombshell side, if you ask me. Besides, she's on the Tazewell board of directors with us. If you showed the least hint of interest, I'm sure—"

He shook his head and angled the phone to show her that the kids were in the room. Beau was not going to discuss dating options in front of Mac and Adele.

She cupped a hand over her mouth. "Sorry," she whispered. "Fine. I wish I could help you out, but this weekend I'm swamped with a work deadline for the application submission, and next weekend I'm already committed to helping the mayor's committee for the festival."

Well, it wasn't like he could switch his assigned weekend anyway. His whole Reserve unit would be gathered for training beginning in the morning at oh-dark-thirty. "Festival?"

"All the hot cocoa you can drink."

Didn't family come before festivals? Yes, but Mayor Lisa Lang wouldn't see it that way. Beau knew better than to request that anyone, even Elaine Tazewell, lock horns with the formidable Lisa Lang.

"Sorry, Beau. But how about this? I'll ask around at the mayor's committee when we meet next."

But he needed a solution in the next half an hour.

They hung up.

Blipping and carnival music of the video game bounced through the room. Beau leaned against the kitchen counter, which still displayed Mom's salt and pepper shakers shaped like little doves. It felt strange to be living here at Turtledove Place, Mom's house—which had been Grandma's house that Grandpa had so lovingly built for her sixty years ago—but without a wife to make it feel like a home. Not that Tracey had been great at homemaking. But still. There'd been a mother *figure* if nothing else.

It had only made sense to move in when Mom died and Beau inherited it, since in the divorce decree Tracey had gotten the house and Beau had gotten the kids.

What Beau should have gotten was a better lawyer.

Maybe he'd been trying to do anything he could to appease her, help her change her mind for the kids' sake. However, within a couple of weeks, she'd visited a tattoo artist and hopped on a rock star's tour bus. Now, she was too busy changing her name and making appearances in glossy tabloid magazines on the arm of that skinny, scraggly musician to even call home on Mac's birthday last month.

Yeah, he'd picked a real winner as the mother of his kids.

Worse, having kids hadn't saved his marriage like he'd hoped. If Mac and Adele couldn't convince Tracey to stay, nothing could. Those kids were golden.

"Daddy?" Mac raced into the room. "Can you help me sing the song for my Christmas program? It's 'Frosty the Snowman.' But I can't remember the words."

Sing?

Uh, Beau couldn't ...

"Mac." Adele marched in, hands on hips. "I'll help you with the song. Leave Daddy alone." She steered him out of the room and toward the dusty piano, where she played a few notes. Not well. "You know Daddy isn't going to sing with you," she stage-whispered. "Don't ask him that. It makes him sad."

Mac shot him a look, but then started up on the lyrics about the old silk hat they found.

With an ache in his muscle at his shoulder, Beau lit a fire in the grate, and then he undid the top button on his light blue uniform shirt and pulled the captain's hat off his head. Might as well give up and call the unit commander's office, tell them he wouldn't make it this weekend.

He'd better find a new nanny. And not one with a libido set to high, and an intelligence level set to nil. Someone with principles. Someone who might learn to actually *love* Adele and Mac.

And fast. Because Beau had pressures of his own. What he hadn't discussed with Aunt Elaine was that if Tazewell *did* get awarded this military contract for the aerial surveillance software they'd been creating and investing in for the past several years, they were set for the foreseeable future. And if *not*, Tazewell Solutions wouldn't live to see another Christmas.

It might not even make payroll to the end of the year.

He pressed the commander's contact and the first ring buzzed.

At the same moment, the doorbell also rang, playing its long, old-fashioned chimes.

The door! It had to be Elaine! She'd changed her mind and decided to work on the application deadlines remotely while she watched Mac and Adele. Beau ended the call, lurched from the couch and jogged to the door. He swung it wide. "Thank you, E—"

The words died, choked off by horror. In the porch light, in a bulky parka and with a large tote bag on her shoulder, stood ... "Tracey?"

Her eyelashes dipped, and he realized his mistake. The younger, much

186

sweeter, purer version of his ex-wife—her baby sister, Sophie.

"I'm here, Beau. If you need me."

Read the rest of single dad Beau Cabot and Sophie Hawkins's story, *Christmas at Turtledove Place,* where Beau gets a second chance at a happy holiday for not just his family, but for his heart—with the one woman he should never let himself fall for.

Author's Note

All stories in the Sugarplum Falls Romance series are clean, standalone holiday romances. **They're arranged in a loop**. Book 1 introduces characters from book 2, and so forth, until *Christmas at Gingerbread Inn* loops back to *Christmas at Holly Berry Cottage*. This means readers can begin at any point in the series and then complete the loop to fall in love over and over, while meeting the many recurring characters from the familiar and charming small town of Sugarplum Falls.

Sugarplum Falls Series

Christmas at Holly Berry Cottage
Christmas at Turtledove Place
Christmas at Angels Landing
Christmas at Sugarplum Falls
Christmas at Gingerbread Inn

Christmas at The Cider House is exclusively available to subscribers to Jennifer's fun, lighthearted newsletter that is a lot more letter than news. Please email Jennifer and ask for your copy at jennifergriffithauthor@yahoo.com. Cheers!

About the Author

Jennifer Griffith lives in Arizona with her husband, where they are raising their five children to love Christmas. She tries to put more lights on her tree every year, and she wholeheartedly believes the best way to kick off the holiday season is to sing Christmas songs with her husband's extended family for two to three hours on Thanksgiving night. Her favorite carol is "O Holy Night," and her favorite Christmas song is "Walking in a Winter Wonderland." She once sang a contralto solo of "Gesu Bambino" that wasn't too bad. The best part of it was her oldest son accompanied her on the piano.

Made in the USA
Middletown, DE
11 August 2024

58912615R00118